PRAIRIE SCHOONER BOOK PRIZE IN FICTION

EDITOR   Kwame Dawes

BLACK JESUS AND OTHER SUPERHEROES

Stories

VENITA BLACKBURN

University of Nebraska Press | Lincoln & London

Acknowledgments for the use of copyrighted
material appear on pages viii–ix, which
constitute an extension of the copyright page.

Library of Congress Cataloging-in-Publication Data
Names: Blackburn, Venita, author.
Title: Black Jesus and other superheroes: stories /
Venita Blackburn.
Description: Lincoln: University of Nebraska Press, 2017. |
Series: Prairie Schooner Book Prize in Fiction |
Identifiers: LCCN 2017005541 (print)
LCCN 2017021174 (ebook)
ISBN 9781496201867 (softcover: acid-free paper)
ISBN 9781496203984 (epub)
ISBN 9781496203991 (mobi)
ISBN 9781496204004 (pdf)
Subjects: | BISAC: FICTION / Short Stories (single author).
Classification: LCC PS3602.L325289 (ebook) | LCC PS3602.
L325289 A6 2017 (print) | DDC 813/.6—dc23
LC record available at https://lccn.loc.gov/2017005541

Designed and set in Whitman by L. Auten.

CONTENTS

ACKNOWLEDGMENTS

There are so many people who have helped influence inadvertently or directly this weird bunch of stories and me as a writer. But I must start with my dear, sweet childhood pediatrician, Dr. Lee. I was a frightfully asthmatic child, lots of hospitalizations, late-night, near-death experiences. At the end of them all were checkups with Dr. Lee and his concerned face. He always told me we have to keep you healthy so you can do all the things you want when you grow up. I wanted to be an astronaut, lawyer, doctor (he beamed at that, which is why I said it even though I hated hospitals), and, of course, veterinarian, actress, and eventually into my teens, a writer. He liked that, and there was something poetic about Dr. Lee even though he didn't say much and spoke mostly with his expressions of worry or delight. But he told me to send him my book when it's done, and I felt that he meant it. That was twenty years ago, and Dr. Lee was retiring then, and I don't know how to find him, but I never forgot.

Now, my people! I must thank my close writing group from early days at ASU, Renee Simms, Dinh Vong Prince, Marqueshia Wilson, and Want Chyi for being so frank and hilarious. Thank you to my new writing buddies Rosalyn Wright and Jen Vargas for helping me realize my dream of starting an official writing community on my campus. Thank you to the Voices of Our Nations Arts Foundation for the encouragement you offer to so many wandering writers of color. A very, very special cosmic bubble thanks to Kali Fajardo-Anstine because of the hope she inspired, having been such a powerful presence when so many of these stories were written. Thank you to Jenni Milton for her wicked sharp insight and to the many editors who worked on these stories with me, as well as my former professors Aimee Bender, Jay Boyer, and Ron Carlson, because they're awesome. And just because . . . thanks to Pam, Deneta, Michelle, and Marcus for being the homies for life, and my family Derek, Donald, Iyanna, Kennedi, Kendall, Kam, Doug, and Venissa.

I'm not the writer I need to be in order to offer thanks to this last person, Juanita Raby Blackburn, my mother. I honestly don't think she would like this book, not enough southern, gothic vampires. Still, she was my best friend and biggest fan. Though she won't ever read it, I hope she would've been proud of me for daring to create something at all.

I wish to thank the following publications for their support of my work:

American for "Scars"
Baltimore Review for "Ways to Mourn an Asshole"
Bat City Review for "There Are No Ninjas in the End"
Bellevue Literary Review for "String Theory"
Café Irreal for "They Only Look Like They're Smiling"
Devil's Lake Review for "in the middle of everything there
    are ribbons of light"
Fast Forward Anthology for "Not Like You, Not at All"
Faultline for "Annie Oakley Gun Training for Women"
    and "Black Jesus"
The Georgia Review for "Ravished"
The Madison Review for "The Hurt Will Make You Stronger"

Pleiades for "We Buy Gold"

Nashville Review for "A Savior, Belief, Tupac, and Balloons"

Nat. Brut for "Barbers"

Santa Monica Review for "Brim"

SmokeLong Quarterly for "Chew"

BLACK JESUS
AND OTHER
SUPERHEROES

BLACK JESUS

After school I arrived at home, took off my shoes at the door, kissed the 8x10 photo of black Jesus in the hall, ate Froot Loops over the sink so Nana wouldn't scream if I spilled milk on the carpet, and then watched TV. I used to watch this cartoon with beasts that turned to stone in the daytime and came alive at night. This was my ritual, my afternoon ceremony of duty, love, and magic. The previous Christmas my Nana came to live with us, my mother and me. In Los Angeles Christmas can be deceiving, but I loved it anyway. I dreamt of cotton snow and the oily smell of plastic holly. Authenticity never made much sense really. All that is real is what is in front of us, if the satisfaction is absolute. Aluminum icicles over the porch satisfied me deeply. Nana, not so much. I killed her, so she says, but she says everything killed her even though she's as alive as a dog bite.

Nana was smaller than me even then, a granddaughter of slaves, and knew life without electricity and frozen waffles. She knew other things too, especially about cows, not just milking them, I'd done that at the L.A. County Fair; she could deliver their babies and cure their sicknesses. When Nana first entered the house she had nothing but her long strapped leather purse, a brick-thick Bible, and that photo of the darkest Christ I'd ever seen. She didn't have a suitcase or anything. I asked my mother, "Why did Nana have to come?" She said, "Your grandmother lived with my sister, and now she lives with us." That was that. "Mama" really is God in the mouth of a child. To her I often prayed on bent knees in the kitchen with knuckles under my chin, "Please, please can I have money for the ice cream truck?" The delicious music of sweet, dairy bliss grew louder. She told me she'd given me enough change the day before, which was true, but I denied it. I pleaded. "No," she said, "I don't want you buying anything from that musky albino." God stirred her pot, and the song passed. When Nana caught me prostrate on the floor, she pulled me up and told me to honor my mother.

Nana and I spent a lot of time together while my mother worked. Well, I spent a lot of time with Nana's rules. One morning she caught me kissing the photo of black Jesus on my way to the bus stop. With her wet, bony palm she slapped me downward on the left temple. I didn't know that much pain existed in all the world. She cursed me dizzy with words I didn't know yet. Then she sat me down and read the Ten Commandments to me in more words I didn't know. I did understand that there were primarily just ten, just ten laws not to be broken. That finite sensibility meant everything to me. I may not have made it through the school day without that number, having been poked with such an emotional ice pick as only my Nana could.

In class I stared at my teacher and wondered. Electricity crackled in my blood and out my ears. She had skin like fabric, a suede eel with really great breasts. Then I knew what I had to do. When I got home I found Nana's mammoth Bible and turned to the book of Exodus and skimmed the commandments. I had to choose one, so I picked "thou shalt not bear false witness against thy neighbor." My Wite-Out pen in hand, I blotted out that commandment and taped another over it: "Thou shalt not kiss black Jesus." It was specific. I was contented. In exchange for the freedom to lie I would no longer kiss Nana's black Jesus.

Several weeks passed by before the alterations to this particular holy text went noticed. Christmas left reluctantly and the Southern California rains came in lackluster sprinkles or vigorous downpours. I'd also discovered a few more transgressions that needed to be included in the commandments. Now I was free to lie at will, covet my neighbor's ass, and completely ignore the Sabbath day as needed. The day Nana found the Post-it note that read "thou shalt not drip milk on the carpet," she roared like a car crash.

"The Bible is God's word," she said, "and God is His word. That's like trying to cover up the Lord Himself. You can't put Wite-Out on God!"

"Then they shouldn't have put God on paper!" I told her.

Nana belongs to the generation of obedience as success and atonement as failure. I belong to the generation of choose your own adventure. Life means adaptation and renewal. I may convert to new faiths. I may travel to foreign communities. My arm may end up in some witch doctor's stew. I may taste like soy sauce and tears. Each cell of the planet may be lovely and terrible, but we aren't afraid to look and see. Nana calmed a little, and we spoke like women. She told me Jesus had copper skin and hair of wool, which sounds a lot like my uncle Sheldon. I confessed my reason for kissing Nana's Jesus. For good luck, I said. I lied. The truth I didn't know how to say then. I'd never kissed a man yet, of course, not a father or a brother or a lover. Kissing that photo meant kissing the best of all men because the best of all men is the one very carefully imagined.

Nana made me fix her Bible for the most part. So the commandments were returned to stone, and I had my ritual. Several winters later Nana isn't able to walk on her own anymore, so I stay by her most afternoons and read. She says I killed her with my defiance. I think I might be stealing her size. I grow bigger, and she grows smaller. When morticians remove organs and weigh them, does anyone measure the tare of the body? What does one weigh without the heart? I'd guess as much as the dead, almost nothing. I read to her from the Bible or magazines or Christmas stories that Nana approves of, but they're never the same when I say them. My mood changes and so does hers. Tonight I tell her, "The crucifix hung from the chimney with care, and Santa's reindeer stood on two hooves with hips jutted to the side in the universal manner of disbelief. Jingle your bells for me, baby; we are all angels." When she is gone I will miss her forever.

BRIM

I'm sure there were errors beforehand—accidental ingestion of household cleaner, a burned palm on the stove, fingers slammed in doors, slips on wet surfaces, a house key in an electrical socket, choking on small objects, near drowning in the tub, and scabs aplenty. I can't speak about those for sure, but I know one incident well, and it was quite the spectacular, tremendous, soul-quivering collapse of good judgment and luck for my family. I was six. Moms couldn't drive for shit. I wish I could say it was a dark and stormy night, but it was a bright, cold, Sunday morning, my favorite kind. It reminded me of the time I slipped crotch down on the exercise bike in the living room and Pops had me sit on a bag of frozen peas. That would've been a day I thought impossible had it not happened. To numb the scrotum via frozen peas is a special kind of euphoria. I wore the hell out of my big boy pants that fateful Sunday morning and ate my entire chocolate, smiley face pancake at IHop. Moms wanted to drive us home afterwards. Pops pushed his lips out and the eyebrows caved in, which meant nothing good, nothing safe. Still, he loved my moms, and that was risky business.

Uncle Dwayne always said Moms had a lead foot. That made me a little proud, proud to be born from a woman with foot bones of metal. I had pride in her feet, at least one of them. My uncle has all of Psalm

139:14 tattooed on his forearm. When Moms caught me writing "one fish two fish, red fish blue fish" on my arm with a marker, she cursed him out mercilessly. Even though Dwayne outweighed her by 105 pounds, she continued. She called him a bad influence, of course, said he should find his own place to live, work more at the tattoo parlor she and Pops helped finance, said he blamed everything and everybody for his mistakes, said he blamed their parents and then the Marines, said she didn't want me to wander through the world blind, breaking things all the time like he did. Moms backed Dwayne into the space between the upright piano and the bookshelf. He flailed his arms and struck her on the lip. Quiet. I heard the house pop the way old houses do every now and then. Moms used her tongue to pull back the blood without taking her eyes off my uncle. They just looked at each other. He didn't apologize. Looking on it now, their conversation didn't seem new. Dwayne's expressions and my mother's violent tongue seemed well rehearsed, somewhat dull to them both. Dwayne's hand was open and rising when Moms was hit, the same way people open and raise their hands to block a glaring light. Both of them told Pops it was an accident. Accident or not, she was right. I did want to follow Dwayne. I would have followed him everywhere. He was always the biggest thing in the room. That meant authority to me, even then, even over my own mother.

Behind the wheel that Sunday my mother stopped being a too-skinny woman with carpal tunnel; she steered like a mad phantom impervious to solid objects and the sorry limitations of a three-dimensional world. Her face offered no emotion. Pops, on the other hand, tightened his body like deadened lobster meat; the terror of mortality widened his nostrils. She half stopped at stop signs. To her STOP meant roll with caution. No other car ever went as fast as we did, even in parking lots. Pops looked back at me. What he saw relaxed him. I suppose that happens when a person witnesses joy undiluted. "You're loving this, Alain," he said to me. I did. I loved the speed. Then our car collided with a news van five blocks from my home. I vomited up what looked like emulsified egg yolk and gutter silt. The impact killed my parents and broke my back. Dwayne and I keep their ashes together on the lowest shelf in the rear of the kitchen cabinet.

It is a bad habit we humans have, doing unsavory things with the dead.

Uncle Dwayne became my parental figure for the next ten years. Being cared for by an adult single man with Posttraumatic Stress Disorder is some exciting and scary shit. Odd alone does not describe the experience justly. Dwayne always lived in our house on the floor in the den, and even after my parents passed, that's where he stayed, leaving the master bedroom unoccupied. He tried to tell me my wheelchair was a spaceship, a time machine, an assault vehicle with semiautomatic weapon capabilities. Dwayne stood six feet five inches and had skin like diet cola poured from a can, full of motion and light. In his head he was a rock star. In front of me he was a Minotaur, hooves and muscle in too-sheer boxers. I didn't just play along for the first few years, I basked in his sudden revelations. He always had big ideas. Once he drained the pool at our house and built a slide for me to go down. The problem was I could never get out of the pool if I didn't have help. One night I slid down on my own, and the thrill of the fall, the independence of being by myself in the dark outside elated me, but, of course, my chair slipped, and I landed on my shoulder. That glorious error allowed me the chance to watch the stars alone for five hours with a fractured collarbone. I thought there would be stars, but the majority of the sky presented just blackness, great and numb and chilled. Only the bizarre passenger jets and helicopters with their goofy dragonfly mannerisms floated under the dark. The eleven-year-old air conditioner whirred then stopped, then whirred then stopped in even intervals. The odor of animal waste is a noble thing, the truest evidence of living. All that evidence of life from the farms miles and miles away and the pets just over the fences nearby collected in a fierce, invisible cloud. The night wind remained callous and inert.

I thought there should be stars as I lay, so I put them there. Only a slight tip of my head could be managed postfall, but that was all I needed to drain the water from my eyes and see clearly every now and again. I filled the sky with whole galaxy clusters. I placed stars at impossible distances right next to the moon and almost the same size, still bright and molten but harmless. My moms used to draw, mostly when she was unhappy. She bought paper but would draw on anything blank and flat. She put glowering faces on the inside lids of my cereal boxes, a warning not to eat too much. She drew on the blank pages of my children's books, always the most unlikely things: enormous fruit with mouths and hands but no eyes, bloated princesses with really small feet and heads, unicorns with steering wheels and tires instead of hooves, toilets with chains over the lid, and pillows with reptilian tails and fangs. I remember laying my books open on my bed to look at the drawings a few years after the accident. That became the day I couldn't remember their faces, Moms and Pops, anymore. I remembered what they looked like in the photos around the house, the same way I remember what Komodo dragons look like from photos and video but not the way they look like lying next to me. I've never met a Komodo dragon, so I, of course, wouldn't remember. That feeling was important, so I told Dwayne. I told him it was like I'd never met my parents. He grabbed my wrist hard and held it a long time. We didn't speak while he held me, but he was angry. Maybe it was the way I said it, almost laughing, I think. I couldn't have been more than ten maybe. Dwayne's forearm tensed, the ropes of veins swelling under the scripture, "I will praise you for I am fearfully and wonderfully made." Narcissists love that; it makes vanity seem ordained, holy. Eventually I cried even though I had no language for the moment, but I understood I was wrong, wrong for laughing, wrong for talking about my parents at all. From then on I left the books closed and didn't consider the ashes.

To me, life after the accident became a ten-year camping trip with my uncle. We had a mystical never-ending supply of canned ravioli and ketchup. The heel of his left foot was blown off, so he walked on the balls of his feet like he was in a production of *Swan* fucking *Lake*. It's dainty. Ten years later we were still together. More than once Dwayne camped out with me in front of the electronics store at midnight, waiting for the release of a new video game. Gamers aren't all black tees and adenoids like Kieshandra says. Gaming is the great equalizer, for sure. Race, disabilities, and that bullshit go out into the wind. For $59.99 plus tax we all become gods of light and destiny, sadistic in our will to see each other subdued.

One morning I came into the kitchen and accidentally rolled over one of Dwayne's precious sketches he let fall on the floor. You'd think I just crushed the head of a new baby the way he reacted. Turns out it was one of Tonie's sketches. Tonie is the big-boobed, hermaphrodite lawyer that co-owned Dwayne's tattoo parlor. She took over the finances after my parents passed. I think my uncle was in love with Tonie, but that goes without saying. Once he was finished coddling that sketch and hissing at me, he went over to the cabinet, leaned his buffalo head down and asked, "What you ever gon' do with this in here that's crowding up the back shelf with all this in here?"

"What?" I asked.

"This in here next to the potato flakes and Vienna sausages on the bottom shelf in here!"

"The potato flakes?"

"The fucking potato flakes. Are you listening to me with the fucking potato flakes? These ashes, Alain!"

He said it like I was supposed to have been working on a plan for the past ten years, and some invisible deadline was fast approaching.

I had no idea what he meant. I had no idea that ashes had to have something *done* to them or *with* them or whatever.

"I'm not doing anything with that."

"Shit."

Dwayne rubbed his forearm and swore again. That was never a good sign. He looked me in the eyes then looked away like he was taking over command of a mission I had no clue was in operation. He had that gleam, another of his big ideas gathered roots in his head and was gonna sprout some fiendish blossom big as my face sooner or later. Of course it turned out to be sooner, the worst kind of sooner.

"Remember I told you Tonie is coming to dinner tonight for a little while because I told you before that Tonie is coming to dinner . . ."

"I got it. I got it."

Dwayne collects ghosts, always has. Even if there were no wars for him, I think he'd hoard bad memories like some dirty cats. He let my parents linger in their bedroom after death. He put their ashes in the one place that gets opened multiple times a day. His bad habit of gathering all the stones of tragedy that should be at the bottom of a lake and counting them made me wary. I figured he wanted to recruit Tonie in his newest plan to pay homage to his sister and brother-in-law, to honor them somehow, to prop up their bones and scream to the world that he's done well. More than that, I knew Dwayne planned to propose. Maybe he planned some kind of farewell ceremony with my parents' ashes and a marriage proposal combination. I actually felt relief knowing that Tonie would be there soon. She calmed Dwayne, distracted him. With her, this next episode could pass smoothly until the next after that.

As a teenager I dreamt of a lot of things. Walking, sure, but I wasn't satisfied with just that. I wanted to run marathon-style over grass rooftops and minefields. I wanted to be as powerful as the elements. I drew my own square on the periodic table: Alaintonium. Symbol:

AtM. When you can't do what other people do, they leave you alone. Isolation is a cesspool for dreams. Mostly I just fantasized about my first pity blow job. This was no girl next door kinda blow job. The girl next to us was Kieshandra McDonough, and she had a nose like a vegetable. This was about her cousin, Michelle, all brown and sparkly. She could've been filled with warm marshmallows for all I knew, but I had her in my thoughts, naked of course, kneeling in front of me while I suddenly have the power to stand. I tell her, it's you, baby, you make it possible. In the dream pink butterflies tumble out of her mouth and elsewhere. When they land on me, they turn to molten steel and sink into my skin. The pain she gives is unforgivable, and I wake up.

That afternoon I sat out on the porch and watched the neighborhood like an old woman. Old women sit on porches and watch memories. Young men with missing vertebrae sit on porches and have visions. In my mind the neighborhood treats me like a sage, telling me their dingy secrets. I listen the way tombstones listen, not hardly. None of that matters because they know I'll be right there later if more needs to be said. I believed in the power of freakish disasters. A man strolling through the woods might be struck by lightning lined with moon dust that fuses him into the trees. He becomes the trees, not just one but all of them, and shares his vagabond spirit with the forest. That moon-dust lightning bolt would fuse me to the neighborhood. I'd be all concrete and aluminum fencing. I'd be a water fountain, no doubt, a badass water fountain, not shaped like me; I'd have a new structure with tiers and spirals, hands of wizards and kings with swords being devoured by multiheaded sea creatures. My whole body tells its story of failed conquest through rebar and stone while toddlers and the elderly throw loose change into my mouth for a better day than the last.

The McDonoughs' minivan pulled into the driveway next door. I flung all hope into the air wishing to see the lovely Michelle, but that wish was shot to ash and debris when Kieshandra stepped out first. I never dream about Kieshandra McDonough. Disappointment is a hollow, hungry feeling. Still, it fades. From the passenger side door came Michelle, turning the air balmy and hazed. The two of them unloaded groceries. Between the shuffle of bags and keys, I noticed that I'd been noticed. Whispers among the girls resulted in Kieshandra moving toward me with a sack of ice cradled under her arm like the result of an unplanned pregnancy.

"Alain," she said, "my cousin wants you to come to this barbecue we're having tonight. You don't have to or whatever."

Despite her sweet potato nose, Kieshandra wasn't unattractive. She had that mock confidence mixed girls get when they think they don't fit in anywhere. If anything, it was her voice that grated on my nerves.

"Tell her thanks."

Tonie arrived as Kieshandra departed. I thought of Michelle's heavy eyeliner that made her eyes so white and wet like the end of a good man's life.

"That must be some daydream," said Tonie.

Tonie, the breastastic hermaphrodite, had a voice light and sweet as cotton candy. She learned to tattoo as a teenager in the Marines. I had a dream once that she crawled on the beach to the shore, lowered her head and drank the ocean dry. Her skin was lit up by the moon, and in the dark I could see whales begin to navigate the blue tunnels of her veins.

"I have a big announcement," Tonie told me, then put a finger to her lips.

This could've been anything from a new car to a baby. A baby seemed a stretch but still fascinating. Dwayne never spent time with children. I thought of a baby Dwayne and came up with just a dwarf-sized version, same dainty walk, same muscular shoulders, same accidental destruction. Tonie asked me how Dwayne and I were getting along lately. I gave her a positive one word response: fine. Fine always meant it could be a helluva a lot better. She knew this.

"They say his condition is normal," Tonie said. "It's a normal response to an abnormal situation."

Her reasoning felt half-hearted, like urging submission to laws she had already broken.

"War is abnormal," I said. "It looks fun until you get used to it."

Tonie leaned against the door frame and gazed out at the neighborhood with me for a while until she had enough.

"You're smart," she said, "and your mother was quite the stunner, if I do say so. Good genes. Gonna make some girl trip all over herself someday."

Then Tonie went inside. Not until I saw her did I even recognize that I missed Tonie. Only a few days passed between her visits, but I liked her there.

"I hope you didn't make that shitty macaroni out of a box again," Tonie said to Dwayne on the other side of the front door.

"You said you loved it the other day when I put the cut-up Oscar Mayers in and said it was special and you loved it."

"You believed me? You think I'm twenty-nine, too, don't you?"

Dwayne seemed to have one foot in quicksand and the other in a pit of snapping turtles. Every direction meant a heap of disillusionment. Tonie's laugh just gathered the reins of one really big and gullible hippopotamus that could kill us all if . . . well, that's just it, if.

At dinner, I sat across from Tonie, who smiled at me. She sat so quiet and still and painted and clean. She belonged in a gilded frame, on the side of a building, in the middle of the Sahara where nothing would dare compete. Dwayne exercised sudden bursts of mania that collapsed the silence with fumbled knives, poorly delivered jokes, fits of coughing, and very loud swallowing. I thought about the morning Dwayne pulled me out of the empty pool. He gave me milk and cereal before deciding to go to the hospital, tried to push the slightly protruding bone on my collar back with a thumb. I don't remember crying. At the table, Dwayne got up to go to the freezer for ice cream cake. Tonie gave me a wink of reassurance. I heard an ice cube fall, then a collision. Dwayne had a miscalculation and hit his head on the freezer door. He made it back to the table with the dessert.

"Alain, I saw you looking at the hottie next door," Tonie said.

"What?" I spurted.

"You were looking at a girl, Alain, a real girl you were looking at?" Dwayne asked.

The awkwardness between us that sat like a fat man on the table started to lose some weight. Dwayne and Tonie now had a common point of interest: effing with me. The two smirked with zero mercy.

"Love and talent are accidental in the celestial dice roll of life," Tonie said.

"Fortune cookie?" I asked.

"Bumper sticker, actually. Have you talked to her?"

"Of course he hasn't talked to her, that would be crazy, right, Alain? Of course he hasn't."

"Why would that be crazy, Dwayne?" she asked.

Tonie's mood shifted.

"You know what I mean it's not you know for Alain because you know what I mean."

The quiet returned, and Tonie was a portrait again for just a flash.

"Dwayne," she said "I want to buy your half of the shop."

"What?!" we said.

Every ordinary thing got really, really loud. The refrigerator vibrated. The air in the vents screamed. I felt betrayed by the basic amenities of life all at once. I couldn't imagine my way out of this. Dwayne planned to make Tonie permanent, and she planned to escape with everything. Honestly, I did not resent her for that. Dwayne rarely worked anymore. Only his name made any appearances at the shop. I was only sixteen, and I knew that a business couldn't be run that way. Then I wondered whether Tonie meant to buy the shop and still be a part of our family as much as she was, but the unsmiling look she had said otherwise. My first thought was to ask to go with her, but that made no sense. She wasn't leaving the city, the state. She was just leaving *our* route to walk in circles without us. She wanted separation, complete and total. Tonie and Dwayne began to argue like two people who have been meaning to have sex but were frustrated because they hadn't quite figured out the logistics. Throughout the battle, Tonie remained her gentle self, always aware of the precarious grasp Dwayne held on right, wrong, and duty. The bruise on Dwayne's forehead turned a color and swelled. I wheeled to the freezer, retrieved a bag of vegetable medley, and put it on the table for Dwayne. They formed an invisible membrane around themselves, so I left the table unnoticed. I did notice the one thing, the one dense, inescapable thing, the collapsed star of normalcy that I thought of as nothing but a weary television rerun. I watched a PBS special about the hormones people unknowingly deposit in the water supply that had been causing frogs to grow enormous genitals or develop organs inside out. Watching shows like that made me feel better and a little proud. I felt better knowing that my life wasn't as fucked up as those frogs', and felt proud knowing how powerful the human species is, how absentmindedly cruel people are to each other and everything else.

When Tonie left, Dwayne became more restless than ever. He walked his dainty walk in manic paths, shaking his head with fury and slapping his inked arms. If he had hooves and horns, he would've gored the wallpaper. It was best to play invisible during Dwayne's fits, but this time he wasn't going to leave me alone.

"Let's go right now; we need to get this done, so right now let's go."

I kept quiet and went along. Dwayne took my parents' ashes out of the kitchen cabinet. For ninety minutes we drove out of the city on I10. At a quarter to midnight Dwayne wanted chicken. In a parking lot, we ate fast food corn on the cob and spat the papery kernel husks out the window. Dwayne taught me a lot of things. He taught me how to patch holes on my clothes, how to mix ink and turn four colors into fifty, how to cripple a man at the knees with a flashlight, and how to survive in this world without living at all. I developed the ability to fantasize with reckless disregard for awakening. There was a bone-white place in between dreams and consciousness, and Dwayne taught me to live there. Just then I tried to think of Michelle and her bright eyes, moving about the party. I wanted to hate her. I wanted to think of her sitting on some guy's lap, hard against her, and his fingers creeping closer, but the vision was broken and pixelated. I looked at Dwayne and saw almost nothing, like seeing the blood in our eyelids. My parents' ashes sat between us in a gray, plastic bag, and I didn't care. This could never be about my resentment or grief. Those belonged to him. I had neither in me. Maybe it is selfish not to feel compelled to honor the dead closest to us, not to feel responsible, at least not anymore. I told Dwayne I needed air, and he helped me out of the car and into my chair. He went back behind the driver's seat, and I began to wheel away. I didn't plan to keep going, but I did, and I knew this was the end of something, something once solid as glass and now gelatinous as memory. You know, family gives you their shit only if you will take it. The oil and grit and brake dust from the highway clung to my wheels then my fingers. On the road the moon ignited the quartz in the pavement, clear and infinite as the stars should have been in the sky.

A SAVIOR, BELIEF, TUPAC, AND BALLOONS

Water balloon wars are primal, vicious productions. Each balloon must be treated with delicacy like a goat bladder, organic, fragile, something sacrificed for the glory of man. The rusty smoke from tin drum barbecue pits makes low-hanging clouds: Independence Day. Faith and Emmanuel were deep in water war. Emmanuel would lose, always bearing the biblical task of martyr, too small. He stops and sits. The long, bony crabgrass reaches out across the porch, aching to touch, be touched, or just acknowledged. He is born an old man, progeria is the diagnosis. Faith is not perturbed. Their friendship exists as all chemical or biological bonds exist, regardless of science or heaven, regardless of belief; they go on like the ants and the snow. He rests and is later smacked in the face, in the legs, the chest, and the ass with hot, wet rubber. M-80s, cherry bombs, helicopters, Roman candles, and all the pretty lights that can burn down a building or tear off a finger scream here is the night.

Faith becomes oddly pretty in a way that makes people wonder whether she might really be ugly. She collects candy, any kind of candy, as long as it has some manufacturer defect. She owned a prized, Siamese peanut M&M, a quadruplet. That one sits in a jar atop a pile of mangled gummy bears, all missing limbs or faceless. The awe of childhood morphs into the horror of puberty. They grow armpit hair, start to smell weird, skunky like sweet smoke and body odor, and fail to notice. Brains get cloudy. Arthritis carves an L shape into Emmanuel's toes. Hair soft as corn silk peppers the sides of his head. He looks like a boy being syphoned away by some invisible gremlin, and no one can make it stop. Faith leaves him for long periods and says you're not going to miss anything. He misses everything. When together, they have the sensory capability to detect only food and rap music. Their clothes are designed to frighten, arouse, or camouflage. Music permeates the house from Emmanuel's room: Tupac, always Tupac. Rhymes of blood, death, and tears beat like an elephant heart in the air vents. Somewhere a hopeless, misguided, futile love persists. Emmanuel turns cruel, ignores Faith when she visits, watches *The Creature From the Black Lagoon* and *The Tingler* on an endless loop. He roosts. There is room for malice in their exchanges. She disappears for a while. Even when present, she is absent. He shrinks into the posture of an apology, and they are inseparable again like a motorcycle and its sidecar.

An accented stranger with a dove-wing tattoo and black eyebrows that sit low like willow branches, interrupts to say hello. Faith hears Jell-O and is amazed. She believes. She marries the stranger, a priest, with whom sex feels like a round of Rock 'em Sock 'em Robots. They knot themselves together with exhausting mental effort. Faith never leaves the city for proximity to Emmanuel. Internal pleasure of being willfully inert is achieved in his presence alone. She makes eggs, snatches candy from her children. Emmanuel rises like a wooden puppet. Cold fingers shock him like drops of water when Faith assists. He curses her strength and takes back his arm. She might have spit on him, kicked him dizzy, and yanked his bones like an irate milkmaid. She jokes instead about lost socks. Clothes go in the washer but never come out. She arches over the laundry and reveals her tailbone and little dimples.

Faith can make babies. Emmanuel bends over like he should be reading a book but with nothing in his hands. Take me to heaven amongst a dying breed, he says. I'm going to fry two extra eggs tonight, Faith says in response. The visits are exuberant at times like a fist to a breastbone. However, on most days the dim rooms indicate somebody must have died. Childhood freedom, purity, and innocence splattered on a tiled floor. The sky is full of orange clouds on one side and clear blue on the other. Cars dump oil like diarrhea. Everyone alive doesn't know something about the people they know best. To the very young and the unimaginative, mamas and papas fall out of the sky, neatly paired up and ready to have kids. No one ever has bad luck or disease that lingers like black slime under fingernails.

The stranger tells Faith and Emmanuel about a trip to pay penitence to the Virgin of Guadalupe. All of the travelers must crawl there on hands and knees. There were fire ants. Everyone stayed really quiet. Bored babies would not remember the quiet or what feels right to adults. Emmanuel declares he needs a new Weed Eater to stop the stranger from speaking. Everybody has a silly little monster that lives in their throat. It never lies. Are . . . are you sick? Dying? Seems the only question he hears, even if the conversation is on water lilies or the Mayans and the Aztecs. The stranger then explains that being a warrior meant you played soccer. They finished the game with their skulls. If you won, then they treated you like a god. The dove wings are completely still. I suck at soccer, Emmanuel says. The little monster climbs up. It's in their mouths. Am I hurting you now? Faith asks about nothing specific. Emmanuel opens a window with difficulty. Giant, black, doughnut stacks of tires stood in rows. The wind makes their sinuses ache. The tires are resilient as if they were expecting it and don't tumble over.

Emmanuel is twenty-eight, a miracle, and a virgin. He carries poems around. People with faces like Faith never live very long, something would happen, someone would happen. There were others—Elijah (the beloved), Enoch (the misplaced), Remedios (the beauty)—all with faces too terrible to bear, faces that hummed, sucked, slid, and scraped against reason, faces for which even God could not wait. Straight into heaven they were drawn, lighter than a falling sheet. She brings him tequila and cola and says the rain is almost here. Her face strikes him, spotted moths fluttering in dark caves where her eyes should be and a hundred more stretching their wings from beneath her hair. He wants to hit her, draw down a yolk of spit and blood. She pops her gum. The stranger is outside in the hall, a dark shadow passes like the back of some giant insect, a beetle, with dips and livable crevices. Emmanuel hums, and the minutelong flash of depravity passes over. They love without bones, snake bodies humming, united as if this and only this will save the world.

Faith is afraid. She dreams often of laundry and assault weapons. She dreams her sweatshirt is flopping through the air, the arms pumping; it struggles but gets going. Airborne. Soon there are a dozen more sweatshirts all different, some have pictures, some have hoods. They flap their arms together and sketch a V in the sky; it looks wobbly for a second, a lumpy U, but then it happens. They get it right, and someone yells "Pull!" Faith's sweatshirt falls out of the sky all popped with holes, the arms folded in the hunch of a stomachache. She wakes changed, altered like burnt paper and knows soon the dream would not be undone or healed over. Emmanuel passes away. Faith is tempted like many to join a lost love by force. She dreams they both drop dead, out of the sky, sitting in chairs with their ankles crossed.

It doesn't hurt, he says, but I'm tired though. The rain falls. A billion little fingers beat a rhythm on the concrete, more complicated than every kind of person. A tinkling lullaby. Emmanuel rests with his hands zipped together and brought to his chin. The half-sewn seam between earth and sky is severed, and the rain makes all sleep.

WE BUY GOLD

Flowers and Eddie became recent regulars at Jonathan's shop. Jonathan treated Flowers like wallpaper carefully chosen by someone else important; while anyone who knew Eddie knew to take him seriously. The shop wasn't always for gold. First there was a haberdasher, then a barber, then a psychic reader, then a watch repairer, and then a dry cleaner. The barber strangled the haberdasher before the courts learned to care. The psychic gave up the shop after finding Christ, only to lose Him soon after. But before that Jonathan raised his family in the city. Compton, California, was neither urban nor suburban anymore. It had stretched out in a flat, wrinkled pattern like an old suit that had been ironed, folded, smoked up, muddied, vomited on, hugged, sold, donated, adopted, washed, and ironed again and again. The city was stylish, young once. Heirs and heiresses to legacies of poverty were born there, sold their birthright, and made fortunes. Somehow the fortunes never came back to the city. No matter how many celebrities gave money or time to afterschool programs, the weary buildings stayed ghostly and unchanged. Jonathan invested in his own business fixing watches. His father fixed watches. His grandfather fixed watches. His great-grandfather fixed watches, and his great-great-grandfather made them. They had a talent for time passed down by mothers and practiced in sons. Watch repair is specialized business, meaning now it's mostly just for fun. After Jonathan's third child with his wife, Azucena, she said no more fun. "Oro, oro, oro," she told him. Gold. The chant, an alarm clock, awakened Jonathan to the prospect of middle-class living. He began buying and selling gold from the shop, and they made money for the first time. In the poor neighborhoods like Jonathan's the signs on the shops were huge and red and yellow and electrifying. In the wealthier neighborhoods outside the limits the signs were discreet and demure, salacious, and platinum.

The last customer of the day, Flowers, entered while Jonathan peered through the layers of magnifying glasses propped up over his work station. Several years ago she vowed never to be seen without nail polish. Her artificial nails arced over her fingertips like the talons of an extinct tropical bird. Flowers and Eddie traveled together. He was the brother of her former lover who snatched chains for Flowers. Eddie was a dwarf with full dexterity in his hands and brown hair. He waited for her outside as usual. Flowers entered with scarcely the sound of healthy lungs and soft-soled shoes. She noticed Jonathan working diligently on a watch and took off her sunglasses. She put them in her purse along with whatever urgency brought her in the shop to begin with. The moment wasn't made for interruptions, for speaking. All of the tools and papers and lights and shelves of cups brimming over with miniscule gadgets fascinated and diminished her. She saw Jonathan's face and witnessed the obligation a man could have to a single, tiny thing, and then it all seemed funny, grave, incomprehensible like a child looking into her father's wallet for the first time.

Jonathan's Doberman remained silent and unperturbed, being one of few species able to recognize malicious intent. Waist-high glass display cases divided the shop in two. Customers remained on one side, Jonathan and his dog on the other. In whatever seconds passed the three of them were content sharing that space in the absence of language. With such a delicate presence added to the shop Jonathan couldn't pull his thoughts away from their usual cliffs. He did not ponder small wires and clock hands. He considered there must be some truth to the talk of heaven. What else keeps humans from running away from each other screaming? If it is love, then why have such a variety? There are parents and children and lovers and siblings. Even a victim is loved by a killer, some version of love that is. Something keeps one sex from overpopulating the other. How do our bodies know when to make a girl instead of a boy or on occasion both at once? If tall is recessive and causes envy, why haven't armies of short-limbed people exterminated their elongated enemies? Why haven't there been centuries without brown hair? These are the things that kept Jonathan awake at night and dreaming in the day.

Hi, she said.

Jonathan dropped a pair of needle-nosed pliers and looked up. She put a clear, plastic Ziploc bag full of gold jewelry on the counter, mostly fragments, gifts from family, some from an ex-boyfriend. With certainty she believed it was all property of the dead or robbed. She was looking to sell, not pawn, which broke the inertia of the hour and made it final. Each piece of jewelry had to be scraped on a flat stone to leave a streak of dust. The dust was then touched with a drop of acid. The pure gold particles shone brightest while the worthless bits of metal dissolved in the clear, wet poison.

The exchange of money for product occurred. Jonathan looked at her license and paused the way most people pause when they see her real name: Flowers Brown. Her parents gave her a name half Disney pet and half Blaxploitation vixen. Anyone called Flowers Brown should spend late nights kicking open crack house doors with buoyant upper breasts exposed between leather hot pants and an Afro the size of all things magnificent and impossible. In reality, Flowers delivered the plain and gentle wherever she went, which is why she was chosen to go in the shop that day. Her parents didn't give her the name they really wanted, something pretty and more specific. They weren't the kind of people who knew the names of plants or how to raise a daughter.

In the bartering Jonathan and Flowers spoke the way best friends speak when they will eventually become lovers then grow so old that the sex they have doesn't look anything like it used to, and in public they still laugh with so little effort that people smile at their marriage with hope and jealousy or mistake them for the special sort of siblings, the kind that are friends. Jonathan complained that his wife won't learn English. She can, but she won't. She watched judge shows on television and thought American women had it all figured out. Her lazy complacency confused him. Then he admitted that he hadn't been faithful to her since their first child, but without his wife he would have been lost. They smiled together. There and just there, desires overlapped. Both wanted freedom that required incalculable steps to achieve. Jonathan's desire to flee the constructs of his life ebbed though he would gladly fix antiquated watches, surrendering to lovely acts of irrelevance any day. Flowers' desire grew in a more steady outward expansion. Then there seemed to be time again. That infinite clock that began when Flowers came in rewound. There was time to hold and be held. He told her she would be happy for fourteen years. She asked if he were a fortune-teller, but he was not. He knew only time. The seriousness in his face made her believe him, and suddenly fourteen seemed frightening. Fourteen consecutive years? The thought of being happy that long without end alarmed her. How would she get anything done? Then the alarm turned to mourning. Fourteen seemed insufficient. Fourteen out of how many more years? Twenty? Eighty?

Cute pic, he said, and returned her ID.

He'd never said that before. Jonathan wasn't tall and had an accent associated with gin-drinking, sociopathic hoodlums in B movies. Still, he had the rare and valuable kind of sexy that men get when their hands can make one thing into another. She asked how long will he be happy? To that he never had an answer.

Thank you, Flowers replied, and left.

If she could have said one thought about the afternoon she would have said, "I'm sorry your dog is going to be killed." When a murderer approaches a dog with a gun, the dog doesn't bark at the gun. The dog barks at the heartbeat, the sweat, and the eyes. This is why Jonathan's dog didn't bark at Flowers. She was just a gun.

Flowers had the bones of a queen and disposition of a fast food drive-thru operator, welcome, what can I get for you? And this isn't because she lacked intelligence or cunning. She needed all of those talents to perform. She simply lacked any will of her own the way blenders lack will when they have no electricity, when they have no fingers to touch the on and off switch. There are people who are always waiting, the way Flowers is always waiting, patiently and harmless until a switch is flicked, and everything inside is suddenly and violently unrecognizable.

The ex-boyfriend slammed Flowers's left hand in his car door to prove a point she already knew. Flowers once arrived late for a delivery, a business deal stalled in the night. Despite her unwavering yield to her boyfriend, his crew accused him of losing control. It was their duty, of course, a chorus of hooded alto-tenors chanting their warrior into action. The boyfriend's duty was to act, pain and humiliation his weapons. Her shame was public as is common for women. He went to prison for something else altogether, but the middle fingernail refused to grow back. Then there was Eddie. He drove Flowers to the hospital the night she lost her fingernail forever in the car door. In the emergency room they made an agreement. They agreed never to like each other but never to leave each other and by any means clip the snags of their existence.

There is one thing truer than most others here. There is one essential thing to understand. Flowers and Eddie came to rob Jonathan.

They came to rob him together. She nodded to Eddie as she walked out of the shop, just a nod. So he went inside.

In his peripheral vision Jonathan saw Eddie and remembered a man who tried to make him laugh. The man said, "So a dwarf walks into a gay bar and says put 'em where I can see 'em. One guy says they're already at eye level." The man laughed and spit and cried a little but Jonathan just wondered. Better, he thought, is if the dwarf plans to rob the gay bar, which would give his statement some credibility. Actually the bar should be next to a bank, so the robber makes the mistake of thinking the bar is the bank. Beyond that the robber should be blind because a blind dwarf in a gay bar is funny due to the fact that populous thinking is crude and insensitive to minorities, gay or little or disabled. Ultimately a blind dwarf goes to rob a bank, but the bank turns out to be a gay bar. The punch line remains unchanged.

Eddie walked into the shop with the deliberate steps of a man carrying a chilled heart for transplant. In his hand where the heart might have been he carried a fast food bag instead. The ubiquitous letter M in the company logo gleamed like godly elbows. Frying starches such as potatoes produces carcinogens, Jonathan thought. Heat oil to unbearable degrees and apply. A harmless, nutritious vegetable is then chemically altered to include a cancer-causing substance. The taste is beautiful, accomplished only through significant damage. Jonathan didn't feel the bullet just the sound, the wreckage of their calm. His dog collapsed on the second gunshot.

Eddie entered the shop and met Flowers's eyes right before shooting Jonathan through the french fry bag. They looked at each other and through each other and somehow beyond all plausible futures with the intensity of a couple considering parenthood at midnight. Somewhere in a city with green hills and no curses they would have many children because Eddie seemed the insatiable type. Their children would be of average height, and in the teenage years one day

Eddie would be lifted from the ground by their oldest son and hugged close, and they would all know the hour they paid for, the grand moment had just been achieved and lost.

Before the light went out of him, Jonathan wondered what could be different. Instead of a gun Eddie might hold a scarab. Instead of being human Jonathan might be a ram, a ram of some impossible color like water or space. Instead of Swiss watches there might be sundials or water clocks, which were notoriously inaccurate: one drip for one second. Flowers and Jonathan looked at each other in the last moments of life and knew they were the same species grown from the ambitions of every other thing. Flowers ushered Jonathan to the altar where Eddie waited, an elevated place for union and sacrifice, a flat rock where the afternoon sun is gentle, and dogs refuse to bark.

THE HURT WILL
MAKE YOU STRONGER

I started to forget the taste of good food since Daddy used to do
the cooking while me and T cleaned up, each body synchronized
in the tiny kitchen, no dish slip, Mama on her ass in the den out
of the way, harmony, nothing but strips of the past now it's just the
three of us—just me, just T, just Mama, a big, white, out-of-order
sign on the front door, all the death food depleted, squash in a can,
which I thought not impossible but a bad idea, especially now the
funeral is long over, church ladies allocating no more scary amounts
of casseroles (noodle casserole, broccoli and cheese, taco casserole,
beef Stroganoff, and the nasty ziti that had no taste at all), marched
dutifully one evening after another until not-anymore arrived followed by get-over-it-already, wherein a mother and her daughters
are supposed to straighten our backs, feed not just ourselves but the
lurkers, the men, the widow vultures all claw and beak, thankfully
of which there existed only one, Pastor Short, determined to come
over almost every day to console us by ignoring me and T completely
and consoling Mama in ways me and T had unspoken orders not to
witness, the longing glances, body grazing, skin-to-skin contact via
cheeks and palms and backs and arms, safe places in theory but in

reality all full of kinky anticipation, which only heightened the unnatural feeling of the Pastor's presence like sitting down to dinner with a five-ton orca in a brown suit, too tight, too square, too foreign, a parody of our family no one laughed at. When Pastor stayed over, the house seemed public domain, impossible to get undressed, wore my jacket and shoes indoors all evening 'til he left, 'til he took his bald, naked, tiny-toothed unconcern for me or T along with the feeling every wall in the house turned see-through, making it hard just to sit down. Mama did come out of the bedroom forgoing her personal weed holidays as T called 'em, not a good thing, just another crack in the house folding up and around us into peculiar structures, not a family dwelling, more a cartoon drawn by a serial killer in kindergarten that he put in the garbage after figuring out that people didn't understand; speaking of serial killers but not really, T told me what we had to do about all of it, about the Pastor and Mama, and the empty in my throat every time I walked home. "We have to poison him or quit softball." Killing our pastor or quitting softball seemed equally gratifying and terrible.

T always knew better than I did about complicated situations, not so much the crushes I would get on other girls, but she understood people's motivations, told me not to trust Mackensie in eighth grade because she just wanted to be my friend for my fruit snacks, Pilar in ninth grade snuck in on my locker space, and now Esperanza inspired reservations. T was always right. I liked that she gave me choices. Quit. Quit? Quit. Quit. Quit. Quit. Quit. Quit. Quit. Quit. Quit. Quit. Quit. Quit. Quit. The word tasted bad, made little since in the context of our lives when Daddy helped us train, sprints every morning, T's shoulders like a fire hydrant, unbeatable fastball, my sprint times unmatched, a duo so good Coach couldn't believe it. He promised to take care of us now, made T break up with her almost-boyfriend, Dawan, a boy too stupid or scared to look grief or Coach in the face without lowering his long duck lips, unlike Coach always there, upright, actually seeing us, and to leave the game condemned us to invisibility, again. T still waited for an answer on killing or quitting, but I took too long to decide, so she hit me on the thigh with a wood ruler, a thick one, didn't make me jump just sent a deep sting through my muscles that showed me stuff, fibers in the carpet crinkling in waves under pressure from the AC vents, some cold and anxious force arced over T, the membrane of fluid around her eyeball deep enough to swim in, asking me for help, and I didn't know why yet, but right then knew for sure we needed to quit softball.

Pastor Short lived on to disturb our house another day, and T so thrilled to be done with softball she actually went to the grocery store and cooked, made me chop the vegetables—onions, crooked neck squash, no cans; she looked the happiest since Daddy died, looked happy all by herself because I did not leap into that pan of joy with her, just gave over the cutting board with all the vegetables, let them tumble into the skillet, oil pop, hot bubble shot onto T's wrist. She said,

"Let's say by some magical fairy dust miracle you are alone with this chick for hours. What exactly are you going to do?"

"I'm done here."

T knew I'd been thinking about Esperanza and how she would take T's spot on the team and how I would never have a real excuse to talk to her anymore now that I left softball and how softball wasn't just a way to keep me and T from being so bored that we roamed the streets and did drugs or made babies; it became this whole person, another thing that was part me, part T, and part Daddy even though that sounds wrong and stupid, truth is softball grew into our group baby, now left on a curb for the crackheads to eat or sell. T just stared at me the way she does when she is serious and not trying to take the blood out of my heart for a laugh, no squint or chin twitch, which gave that away.

Daddy encouraged the competition between me and T, invented our first game while we exercised in the garage with tiny, pink weights heavy as a man's shoe; when lifted the way he told us felt like dancing, bend up then down, pass one to each other, back around again, then rest the muscles so they heal from the hurt and get bigger, better. One time Daddy flew across the country when Uncle Samuel died from a MRSA infection, leaving Mama to take care of us alone. She knew about our games, had another one in mind Daddy didn't know about, boxing, where we put on oven mitts for gloves, mine pink with burns, T's the good red ones all new, waving from her corner of the living room, me in the other, listening to Mama's whisper, told me T thought she was prettier than me, smarter than me so forget about a win because I could never beat her at anything, said something to T, too, that I couldn't hear but didn't matter after a few minutes when the anger heated the room, heated my hands with the belief Daddy talked to T more, thought she knew more words than me, words I might not ever know, making sense of the hate under those circumstances, hate for the burns on my gloves, hate for being shorter, dumber, so when Mama yelled fight! I ran to T's corner and wailed on her 'til the mitts fell off, our fists and faces shellacked in tears, spit, stoppered by a promise not to tell Daddy because Mama said he'd be angry that we couldn't keep the mitts on like the professionals, her deception now our own.

Mama must've smelled dinner to decide on emerging from her hot box bedroom, a peek out into the light of the kitchen like a witch behind a tree in a forest of smoke to examine the work of her minion, one pinch of squash, a chunk of cornbread, then an idea bent a smile into her cheek muscles, one I already knew coming, deflated my secondhand happy before the order leapt off her lips. She wanted us to cook for Pastor.

Into my consciousness Esperanza Duarte brought echoes of sherbet ice cream, baby llamas, refrigerator magnets, high scores, beating T to the first pancake off Daddy's grill—my escape from T and Mama, antlers locked over the macaroni salad, just enough carrots in my opinion, though T wanted more the way she wanted more out of Coach, his smell the only sensible thing about that relationship, beautiful, cinnamon toast in a lumberyard while everything else felt like one of those things people accept if they don't think about them at all like other planets, cell phones, mouth bacteria, identical triplets, the beginning of earth or the end; a happy thought in a girl with absurdly long legs who made terrible expressions whenever faced with a camera, destined to do some injustice in numerous ways, eleven exactly in my possession, eleven terrible photos of Esperanza, crooked smiles that didn't quite open on time and shadows that made her face look skeletal or bearded.

Pastor sat at our table the way he had when all of the death food lingered, part owner, confidant, poser, an understudy. The laborious circumstance of eating with him increased one thousand percent because T and me did the cooking, every bite he took cut into something we made, something we shaped out of something else more inferior. Smack. Swallow. Spittle wipe. An animal, a lion eating a cub that did not belong to him, Pastor dared say my name when I did not expect it, causing my fork to slip into a not subtle clatter, debris across the table, on Mama's lap, and ended in a decrescendo on the laminate below, T's look of amusement and disgust as if I had lost an ancient battle by falling off my horse in midcharge, unforced error.

Esperanza arrived first at the party, alone, hunched over as always because she must not have mirrors in her house to know beauty is supposed to be straight, unaware of her own body and what it meant to the world, brushed her forearm against me when stepping inside, earning my eternal devotion, an offer, a blood sacrifice of all I own/ love in the form of a cold soda T suggested adding rum to, which I refused. The team filed in.

My battle ended in a loss, a scream of metal on my plate, then the floor while Pastor and Mama remained simply ogre and witch, nothing too tragic or dangerous, like they existed for T, a dangerous opportunity that I didn't recognize.

If Esperanza thought dead kittens pretty, I would've murdered my neighbor's Scottish fold and delivered it in an Easter basket, green and purple plastic grass, evidence of my obsession evolved into socio-pathic inclinations (for her alone), but thankfully, Esperanza liked lemon poppy seed muffins and healthy cats instead, talked about her grandma's sixteen-year-old Himalayan for eight minutes before Coach showed up. Coach didn't stand much taller than the boys our age, but what he lacked in height he made up for in width, narrow waist with cartoonish shoulders, the image on an action figure box all the boys aspired to resemble except for the receding hairline, saggy undereye skin, and baby jaw. During the party he and T went into our bedroom alone with me under orders not to let anybody in even though Mama lounged about in her bedroom, door shut, having also told me not to let anybody in, both of them under the impression I cared about the party or keeping it down or turning it up or Coach at all or how he couldn't make T break up with Dawan if she didn't want to or T being a virgin before that party and not after when their tiny tug-of-war couldn't pull our house down unless Mama cared. On paper she ruled.

His second helping of cobbler revealed that Pastor Short, though he laughed and ate and spilled the appropriate scripture and condo-lences from the wet corners of his lips, had nowhere to go, waddling in his happiness right there in our house next to Mama's, too, a pleasure tucked deep in our collective mourning worthy of hatred for intruding, for insulting my father without words. He seemed only half man again but less organic than a whale, clownish, mechanical, powered by the weakness of my mother that wouldn't allow her to be alone with me and T or herself, full of programmed phrases like the robot singing bears at kiddie pizza restaurants.

T wanted the poison, her time in the bedroom an outright rejection of possible peace with Pastor Short, the purple robot bear that had sex with our mother too early at night and sang hymns of Christ's everlasting love did not suffice. I stood in the hall between bedrooms, exhilaration taking hold because I stood away at a safe distance, away from the risks T made with Coach, the things he would introduce her to (manual shift transmissions, Hennessy, the human papillomavirus, an obsession so piercing it looked like religion) to hurt back our mother because though they hurt me they hurt each other more. The power soon stretched into agony as I remembered the blood obligation of a child to a parent, sister to a sister, helpless in either since, a lost sensation like a toddler wandered off in a store, confused, convinced of eternal isolation. Esperanza smelled like old pennies and orange juice, leaned against the wall next to me, side by side, before I saw her approach, both unwilling to speak, allowing me a few minutes off duty away from the tasks, every chore assigned to me without my approval, affording a day of rest concentrated into a few breaths to think of love, which was never the problem only the truth about more after love that must come, the unwinding of strings, threads busted, matted like dog fur on a blanket rolling around on hot in a dryer, an undoing big as death/divorce, maybe love that blossoms then rots in seasons; it frightened me.

CHEW

We chew in our family. It's our God-given freedom to chew what and when we want. I chewed the legs off my grandmother's piano. It keeled over and crushed her thirteen-year-old bichon frise, Ginger-snap. My granddaddy laughed his ass off. Me and my brothers used to chew shapes into things all the time. We turned straws into palm trees. I made a lily out of a milk carton for my brother's girlfriend. I had to be careful around the seams and not use too much saliva or it would've turned to oatmeal. He busted my lip for that one. My boy is just like us, can't keep his teeth off things. He chewed a plastic coin into a funny shape and supposedly threw it at some girl. They suspended him for two days for a plastic coin. I had to sit in front of the superintendent with his blood-red hangnails while he read off a statement from a teacher. "Because of the zero tolerance policy, suspension was warranted after the disruption caused by the object. The student chewed a coin made of plastic until it resembled a bullet and threw it" yada yada "while yelling bang, bang" blah blah "repeatedly until the situation escalated" or some garbage. I had to sit there for thirty-nine minutes looking at that shitstorm of a desk. It was metal and the color of every dull memory I ever had, just covered in papers, papers, papers. He held his palms above the papers and patted the air as if disgusted, as if afraid to touch anything because he knew it all linked to him somehow. One wrong move would topple it, and he'd be late for some god-awful appointment or something. I told him to let's just get right down to it. He sighed like he'd heard the story a few too many times, from the teacher, from the principal, from that big-haired news anchor, and his own bosses probably. Still he needed to hear the story right from my boy. So that's what happened. My boy told the truth of it. I told my boy to be out with it, and he stayed quiet because kids don't know what to say without a question. What happened? I asked. "I chewed a shape the teacher thought was bad. She made me go to the principal, then she brought all my stuff and called you, Dad, to come get me." That's what he said. The superintendent dared to look at me like I coached him, like my boy is just so acutely aware of my breathing and knew every inhale and internal body gurgle and could tell the good from the bad. How is he supposed to know what gesture meant certain doom and which meant good job, son? But he said it right anyhow, "I never threw it at no one." My boy told me about that crooked-eared girl who teased him all the time about his dirty cuffs. I told him never wash your cuffs for a girl. If she can't love your grease and grit, she can't love you. Well, he washed his damn cuffs and got more teasing for the trouble. That's when he chewed that shape into the coin and supposedly threw it. I knew he wasn't trying to make a bullet and pretend to kill that girl. That's crazy. I told him to tell that pudgy superintendent what he was really trying to chew into that fake money, "I was trying to make a rocket. I chew rocket ships and I like guns and tanks and I was just trying to draw a rocket but it turned out to look more small like a bullet than like a rocket, and the teacher just thought it was a bullet." The teacher just thought it was a bullet. Boys that age chew all kinds of things. I must've chewed a cock into the side of a cereal box a hundred times before I knew what it was for. Boys just celebrate themselves, you know. It's human. But the superintendent didn't get it. He just sat there on his secretary's wide wood chair thinking, "*Your boy is an unholy wretch that will grow up to hurt people. The world is going to have to kill him someday. He'll embarrass you and drive you indoors for good. You are an enabler. You think you're helping, but you're reinforcing terrible behavior. There are volumes of books written, studies done, talk shows even about you and your boy. There will be nowhere safe to drive to except hills with no life on them.*" The superintendent blinked. He looked at my boy and blinked. He looked at me and blinked. He looked at the stacks of pink and yellow papers, folded and crinkled, some thin as spit, and blinked. What right did he or anybody have to judge me and mine? They call it enabling. I'm enabling my son to keep on with his bad behavior. They just don't understand our lives. Maybe he did chew a bullet on purpose, and throw it, and push her down, and kick her until she cried. We all chew to survive in this world. My granddaddy chewed up until his last days on this earth, a little foil applesauce lid. He made a teacup for my grandmother. I heard she told him to swallow it for being such a mean bastard all his life, but that's just how they loved each other. Everybody else can't know what it's like to put something in your mouth and have something different come out, what it means, the power. They just want to take it from us, keep us docile like starved dogs. They don't know anything about how we live, love, and die. My boy is innocent. My boy is gifted.

TAKE ME TO THE WATER

Nasty Nicki came to my baptism. True shit. She had that beautiful body, always made me think of nectarines and half dollars under a face like hell, invisible, nobody could look right at her without feeling too much. Like how your stepmom was way too old for your dad. You were my mirror then. I weighed our parts, grams and pounds, a milliliter of breast to an ounce of penis. (Which is heavier? More useful?) I knew the burden in carrying around boobs all day, a worry and duty you and the boys did not have. We listened to those Sam Cooke songs on the way to church and pretended we didn't like them and couldn't get 'em out of our heads, and I always thought of Nasty Nicki. After church, you'd let me wear one of your hockey jerseys, even though we didn't give a fuck about hockey, my body happily lost in the oversized clothes, more you than me, and we'd take the bus to Santa Monica where no one knew us.

Nicki doesn't walk the grid on Central anymore. Gone. No, not long-trip gone. Rot and bones gone. I miss her even though I can't half remember what she looks like, never heard her say more than hey nigga, hoping to get a dollar out of me. Others more cracked out than her moved in, younger, all smaller than actual people but with the same shape, like something made in a lab, a big experiment all fucked up, left for us as a reminder like the ghosts in Pac-Man. They chase the mouth that eats the balls of light, and somehow Nicki was the ghost and the mouth. I don't know about the lights.

Before the actual day I didn't care one way or another if I got baptized. It was all a pageant, poor hood-style kabuki theater of gods and men, but Nicki made me believe in the water. She made me believe that I could undo everything, everything before and after just by dunking my head under for a few seconds. I could bring her back to life, feed her with my whole soul. They played Sam Cooke at my baptism. I know that's impossible. The choir must have sung the usual hymn about being led to the sea or a river or a lake, swelling with messianic redemption. They couldn't have played a song about being in love with a woman. Still, I see Nicki there in her long T-shirt, a junkie hooker's ball gown, no pants, no skirt, no panties, legs out in the sun, watching me walk down the aisle draped in white baptismal robes, smiling at me like she had a secret, like together we would crack the cocoons frozen around us, remake the earth, like we might be there in that space of light forever.

IN THE MIDDLE OF EVERYTHING
THERE ARE RIBBONS OF LIGHT

1,277. That's how many hairs are on my arm, I tell the doc, up to the elbow. The doc looks up at my wife and me. We both had that bruised cantaloupe feeling you know. At one point everything is just right, and then it all falls off the counter. Your daughter is special, he tells us. My baby girl never liked men in white jackets. The doc's collar is always bleach bright. His bottom teeth show when he talks, too, so I don't trust him either. We knew autistic meant you got a bad vaccine and will never make friends. The doc tells us we're wrong in every way. Have you heard the term idiot savant? he asks. My wife stands up, bones on fire mad. She's big as a ten-year-old boy with a crocodile soul, snaps hard at the whole sky sometimes. Once at a traffic stop I hit the brakes too hard and some poor dummy slammed into me. Well that poor dummy got out of his truck with a twinkling baseball bat. Before I could speed off quick, my wife jumped out with nothing but her flip-flops and a mouth. She spit all hell and unholy mischief and disparaged that poor dummy back into his little truck. Your daughter is gifted, the doc says. He talks lizard legs quick to calm my wife. He didn't mean idiot like poor dummy. He meant my baby girl has special abilities. Can she bend spoons and shit with her thoughts? my wife asks. No. I knew that. When my baby girl counted my arm hairs, I knew she got it right. She had that look that was all business, and it scared my wife. So we have to talk to men that me and baby girl don't like. My baby girl likes to count and not much else. She told me numbers have colors and shapes. She said every single thing looks like a number. I'm 117. Apples are 88. My wife is 9 and 26. She got to be two numbers because she changes. Baby girl said everybody's number stretches out like a shoelace or a bowtie and bounces back. Sometimes the number is so bright she can't stand it and cries. I guess that's why my wife is scared. When we weren't looking someone we knew counted up the whole world, saw inside each bit, and it was nothing like we thought it would be.

STRING THEORY

I did not speak until I was six years old. My laugh was pretty as new chalk, I've been told, and I attempted time travel at age twenty. We met in college. It was the first week of fall classes. I sat as usual between two empty chairs in the front row of the room. The professor, a mid-twenties, tenure-track phenom not yet jaded by the academic institution frequently referred to as "the tar pit," prepared to take attendance. His slack-jawed yet earnest response to every less than intelligent question endeared him to his students.

"Welcome again to Quantum Physics," said the professor.

I loved math but liked to ask too many questions. Math requires acceptance, and I was too often compelled to ask why and how. I think I'm a philosopher and a mathematician. Only the theorists allow for both. Though difficult to say from just my facial expressions at the time, this was my favorite class. This might be even more unbelievable considering I passed out in my chair and collapsed onto the floor the second day of the semester. On the first day the professor presented a 3D slide show on the theory of black holes, after which a young man inquired about the location of the nearest Applebee's. The remaining seven minutes of class involved determining the fastest route to that particular restaurant. On that second day, however, the class paid more attention. That discussion did not end well for me. My mind wandered as I've been told it never should be allowed to. Only two other times has that happened, once just a few years earlier.

When I was a junior in high school, my earth science class spent a month discussing nothing but climate change. In my memory now the instructor is only a viscous blot of purple jelly with a voice like a public service announcement. There is one day in particular during class that changed me forever.

"You all might find this hard to believe," said the Blot, "but the moon, as we learned, is a vital part of Earth's development. Believe it or not, the moon is gradually moving away from us."

I stayed alert during these classes and wrote notes quickly, almost verbatim, but this announcement made me stop.

"That's right. During early Earth the moon was much closer and the days much shorter and hotter, but fortunately for us the moon kept spinning much like a pendulum in reverse. Instead of the rotations becoming shorter and shorter, they grew wider and wider. The days became longer, giving the seasons time to develop and life as we know it the chance to prosper."

This idea had a profound effect on me. I cried. As if in response, the Blot continued on like some sadistic emotional parasite, draining the fragile contentment from my body. The fixed and true universe I knew suddenly felt fraught with a violent uncertainty that I could not control and did not want to consider. To calm down, I wrote the number one followed by a zero, then another and another without stopping.

"Can any of you guess the repercussions of such an event on the Earth?" asked the Blot. "Longer days, yes, but without seasons, without tides. The Earth will slow down, and if the Earth slows down the planet will get superheated in some areas and frozen in others."

Shoulder-heaving sobs escaped me, and a few of my classmates noticed, concerned but too curious to act.

"There is a good side though," said the Blot. "This will take billions of years to happen, by then the sun will have already eaten the Earth in its fiery last stages of expansion before death."

The bell rang to signal end of class, and I collapsed. I began to regain consciousness while being taken down the crowded hall. The students who had noticed my sobs held me by the elbows while the Blot occasionally shouted "get the fuck out of the way" or "goddammit, move." By the time I fully gained consciousness again I was not in high school anymore. I held a paper cup of water in my left hand and sat up in a chair in my quantum physics class. The professor and Mariko Lee crouched in front of me. Mariko's face had the shape and depth of a leaf. Her presence was that of a very large man even though she was only big enough not to be a little person. Her wrists were a mystery.

Something happens to people who rescue other people, a covenant of sorts. The danger can be big or small, dragging a man from a burning car, plucking a fish bone from a toddler's throat, or giving water to one who is thirsty. The promise is the same: when I see you, I will keep you safe. I looked at Mariko, the quasar of freckles between her eyes, and that promise was made.

Today Mariko entered the class trailed by her boyfriend, Alkie, just as the professor neared the T's on the roster.

"Miss Lee and Mr. Brooks, welcome," said the professor.

Mariko always entered a room like some fairy tale heroine whose mission is not half done. She always spoke a little too close to people, but because her eyes were black and her shampoo pleasant no one stepped away. She wore a satin ballerina outfit with matching slippers and white stockings along with an oversized, dusty, black gym bag. Something wasn't quite in order: her face. There was a half-moon bruise along her cheek and a puffed lip with a slit of red and green on the right side. The swollen lip made her look catlike and dangerous. Beauty had eaten the beast and made a pretty monster.

Even with that facial damage, Mariko's powerful presence had not diminished. She and Alkie eagerly took the seats on either side of me. Mariko even smiled in my direction. I did not smile back. In the moment after, Mariko lifted her hand to her mouth, decided against touching it, and turned away.

During the forty-minute lecture, I dictated every word the professor said except for "the," "an," and, of course, the "ums," "ahhs," and "errrs," which occurred on every twelfth or nineteenth syllable. When the professor concluded, I also wrote the numbers 4 and 436 in the margins. Each represented the number of times Alkie stealthily scratched his genitals through his jeans and the number of breaths Mariko took during the lecture, respectively.

"Now you all need to take copies of this before you begin the group activity on page 17," said the professor. "There is a $5,000 prize at stake for each of you in the physics department. You can work together outside of class as a group, but only one student can enter and win. The contest is simple. Create it or prove it. Come up with a new theory on the function of the universe as we know it or prove a theory already in existence. Submission deadline is November. Now get to work on page 17, so we can review."

"Looks like we're a team today," said Mariko.

With all the gauze stuffed under her lip, it looked like a lacerated caterpillar was trying to escape in between words. Alkie laughed and shook his short dreadlocks. He had a Caribbean accent and smelled like blueberry hookah and popcorn. We were the same color, oxygenated apple meat. We could have shared a skin.

"Shut uff," Mariko told Alkie, then turned to me. "I know I sound terrifle. It haffened at fractice. I'f just starting, so I need to fay fore attention. You fust think I look awful too?"

"No," I said. "It just seems that ballet is dangerous business."

Alkie let out a laugh loud enough to quiet the room for a few seconds. Mariko smiled in pain as well.

"Fallet class is this afternoon. I had fixed fartial arts this forning."

"Mixed martial arts," said Alkie. "She wants to be an Ultimate Fighting Champion. Good luck."

There was little confidence in Alkie's tone. I did not laugh, only nodded. Mariko leaned in closer to me, far beyond the ordinary uncomfortable distance she normally maintained with people.

"We saw your name in the Student Daily this morning," she said. "You're Reese Fairmont, a Presidential Scholar?"

I confirmed.

"Whew," Alkie whistled. "That's really phenomenal. Full ride, plus you stay in those swanky dorms."

"My sister was one three years ago," said Mariko. "I only got 50 percent tuition waived. I might earn an athletic scholarship."

"Title IX whore."

Mariko gently stabbed Alkie with her ballpoint pen. No penetration. She began to study the contest flyer intensely. In the close proximity I saw that no matter the devastation to her face Mariko would always be lovely. I would not be pretty for another four years, and even then it would last only six. Mariko touched her tongue to the green stitch just above the gauze and crossed her legs with the grace of a calla lily bending in the wind.

"Those skank ballet twats kicked me out of the club!"

Mariko stomped, slammed, and screamed herself into the living room of her on-campus apartment where Alkie and I waited for her to join us. This was our first meeting to decide what to submit for the theoretical physics competition.

"They said my image is 'too brutal for this delicate endeavor.' Well those asshole tongue fucks can suck it! What's the matter with you two?" asked Mariko.

There must have been something peculiar in our demeanor, mostly Alkie's, for mine did not change so dramatically. Before

Mariko arrived, Alkie in his island voice full of careful vowels and half-hearted consonants asked: How are you? Where did you get that belt? Why don't you talk more? Do you think Mariko is crazy? Are you hungry? To which I replied: Fine. My father. I don't understand. The possibility exists for us all. And no, not at the moment.

He wanted a peanut butter and plantain sandwich, so I waited on the couch while he went to the kitchen, which was just another part of the living room. I could see him operating over the bar used to divide the space. With his side to me I could see him slice the plantain. He held the fruit and knife close to his chest like he was breast-feeding a small animal with ill-designed man nipples. With his sandwich in both hands he took a deep bite and exhaled heavily through his nose. The sound was that of water and air like a faucet shuddering on after a long time off. Before that bite reached its natural end, another and another collided. Alkie put his hands on the counter and worked nothing but his jaw to free the roof of his mouth of that gummy clog. Soon his knees bent farther, and he coughed the way one does when peanut butter touches the lung. He eventually pushed himself upright again, his triceps vibrated like a strummed guitar. It was a desperate act, hurried and impatient. When complete, there seemed little gratitude, as if the food were never there, never there at all. He then moved slow and contented while he made another sandwich, as if the room were filled with invisible smoke and water, everything sweet, everything salty. I know now that it meant happiness. Alkie brought the second sandwich and offered it to me.

"Now I get to watch you eat."

He smiled and placed the food on the coffee table next to a box wrapped in a patchwork of black construction paper. With his index finger he lifted my entire hand and moved it a little closer to the table. Instead of the sandwich I reached for the gloomy box, but Alkie moved it away.

"You don't want to look in there."

His mood changed so completely that I noticed new colors in the room, a lime-green lamp that burned hot in the corner, purple and orange paisley prints on the rug. Then Mariko came home.

"We were just waiting for you," said Alkie. "I guess this means cello lessons in the afternoons?"

"Fuck a cello," she replied.

"Sounds complicated."

"I'm sorry. I'm just so angry."

Mariko cast her body down in front of me with her chin to chest, ready to be smote or knighted or held. Her genuflections often came that way, sudden and unwarranted. She hugged my knees and put her head in my lap. I did not hold her or stroke her hair or tell her that the world hurts sometimes but we all get through it. I didn't know that was expected. Mariko eventually sat back on her heels.

"I had a fish once," she said. "I loved to pet him. My mom told me not to do it because he wouldn't like it, but I didn't believe her. I had to pet him. He felt nice, too, smooth like jewelry. I rubbed his side every day after school. He got patches and died. His name was Jennifer."

Mariko looked at me with such sincerity and understanding that I almost touched her.

"That story was so fucked," said Alkie. "I hope you never had a puppy. Jennifer? It's all so very fucked."

Mariko looked at Alkie then at the uneaten sandwich and back to me.

"I'm glad you're here," she said. "Did you eat? No? I need cheese and bread."

"Frozen or delivery?" asked Alkie. "Oooh, I have an idea for the competition!"

Alkie rushed back around the bar to get an apple from the kitchen. He paused in front of us and held the apple out at his side. He let it go.

"With bacon," said Mariko.

"Don't you get it? Relativity! We'll do something to prove it, debunk it, expand it."

Mariko turned to me and asked if I had any pizza topping preference. I asked for olives.

"What is wrong with relativity?" Alkie asked.

"Nothing," said Mariko. "That's the problem. We are not going to win the most prestigious award in the whole department by boinking around with outdated theories. Let me go check in the textbook. There might be some inspiration there. Don't forget the olives!"

Alkie went into the hall to phone for pizza, and Mariko went into her bedroom to retrieve her physics book. I reached for the little box on the coffee table. As soon as I lifted it, the contents began to escape. Gray sand sprayed the table and rug. I acted with more care. Inside the box the sand reached the top of the lid with a corner of white paper semisubmerged like a bottle in the ocean. I pulled the paper only to see the bleak remains of a photo folded over and over like a riddle. The image had deep crevices cut along the heads. They were all Mariko's head but not hers completely; there were a man, a woman, and a young woman who appeared as fun house versions of the actual Mariko, diluted by light and mischief. All of the dreary contents I returned to the box.

Just over a week later Mariko and Alkie arrived at my parents' home to work on our submission. The home I grew up in was beautiful with bay windows and a peach tree thirty years old. In between its initial planting and my family's arrival, the house endured a termite infestation, raccoon nesting, the neighbor's garage burned down, three separate gangs claimed the street as territory, the other neighbor's home was converted into a crack house, two recessions, and a flood. My mother and father opened the door with the same interest in their guests as they might show a pair of butternut squash. Mariko, however, entered as though she might bear hug my father around the waist. My mother insisted on sitting down to a snack.

Mariko: We're lucky to have Reese as a partner. She's brilliant.

Mariko took a bite of a generic brand vanilla sandwich cookie.

Mom: Reese never had many friends.

Mom did not eat.

Alkie: That presidential award is hard to get. Only three in the entire entering class are awarded.

He pushed an entire sandwich cookie into his mouth.

Mom: Reese never had a boyfriend.

Alkie inhaled a crumb from his sandwich cookie and gagged.

Dad: Have you been taking your meds?

Dad tapped his cookie on the tray like a cigarette.

Me: Yes.

Dad: No episodes?

Me: Not for a while.

Dad: . . .

He opened his sandwich cookie carefully, as if the truth lay inside and might be damaged if handled poorly.

Mariko: Um, I'm trying for an athletic scholarship. No one in my family is good at anything like that.

Mom: Reese never played sports.

Me: Let's go to my room now.

They say parents are the mirror in which we glance to determine our whole value. Perhaps that is true enough. I've always thought of that green paste dentists use that dulls the pinch of the actual shot just a little. Soon the paste has no effect as the needle enters the quick of the gum, the crunch of the nerve and the spill of medicine turn half the mouth to meatloaf, dead and warm. To my parents my own nerves were the enemy and had to be battled with vigilance. Some of us feel everything more than is reasonable. I remember being very young. I laughed at cartoons and sometimes commercials with animals in pants or hats. I would laugh so hard the room changed colors, and I'd vomit. The sound of crickets made my eyes jitter and caused headaches that lasted for hours. Every part of the world had a song and screamed it over my shoulder. The doctors gave me pills then. The doctors gave me pills that made me sleep eighteen hours a day. They gave me pills to teach me to speak. They gave me pills to make the other pills work. The doctors eventually found the combination of drugs to make me closer to everyone else. The sounds of insects in the nighttime didn't hurt anymore, but the color of people's tongues couldn't make me laugh. When the pills took my skin and wiped the bare muscle and tissue with that green dentist paste, everyone seemed satisfied. I refused my medication only three times, once in high school, once before this semester, and once before attending an all-girl cage fight.

Just the two extra bodies in my bedroom made the space lose all right angles. The walls and windows seemed more like domed glass, and the three of us confined in a snow globe. Mariko and Alkie leaned in on me, their knees almost on my shoulders asking me questions about my medication, the dosage, the cost, to which they mostly replied, "Wow, that's a lot." Soon Mariko found the conversation dull and took out her phone and checked a message. She had good news to share from her coach. Her first qualifying mixed martial arts match would take place in a week. She delivered a jab-uppercut combo to the air. Alkie made himself comfortable on my bed, and Mariko flopped down on his lap. She had to share the good news with her family and called home, but her sister answered.

"Put Mom on the phone . . . Just do it! . . . Where did she go? . . . Well, I have good news . . . No, I didn't get the scholarship yet, but I'm close . . . I have a match next week . . . Not ballet, you . . . I had to quit ballet! . . . I know she wanted . . . Can I finish please?

Thank you. The match is next week, and I want you guys to come . . .
yes, *you* too . . . what . . . of course he's going to be there . . ."

Just then Mariko put the backside of her knuckles to Alkie's cheek
and showed more tenderness than I had ever seen between two living
people outside of movies and TV. Still, their faces were not of happy
lovers climbing the soft hills of romance together. I realized someone
thought their affair unreasonable. Like so many other things Mariko
was told to leave alone she couldn't resist. Alkie wasn't the type to
get patches and die. He could be petted freely. Mariko proved that.
She counted him a victory when those dearest could not. The two of
them sat on my bed with the look of a couple scaling Mount Everest
in tank tops and Bermuda shorts, Sherpa-less.

"I have an idea for the competition," I said.

Mariko stood up and came to me without a word as if she'd been
waiting for this, as if the lives we lived apart were just bad movies
that were finally ending, as if we were fugitives from other worlds
trapped on a cruel planet, as if together we might now go home.

I told them about strings, about the little vibrating bits of us all
inside of every atom, inside of everything. Each moves at its own
frequency but they are all the same, revolving belts of energy. In
theory we can't prove they exist because our technology can't see on
such a micro level yet. I proposed we design a program that could
see for us. The idea was half science, half fiction, and all Mariko
could have hoped for.

"I need to use the restroom," she said. "I'll be right back. You just
tell us what you want us to do."

Once Mariko left the room, Alkie pulled me toward him away from
the door the way secret keepers do when the secrets can't be kept.

"I think she's going to ask you to let her submit the project in her
name."

"You think I should let her?" I asked.

He shook his head furiously, the scent of blueberries everywhere.

"You should do what you want. Mariko has her reasons, but you should do what you want. You could do a lot with that money." He looked around. "Your family could."

Mariko returned.

"What are you two up to?"

"You ask that a lot, you know that," Alkie replied.

Mariko's cage fight took place at a small downtown arena that smelled like midsummer public transportation. A wire fence fifteen feet high, no different from any low-grade street fencing, surrounded the center ring. Mariko was scheduled to open for the main event between two fat-free men resembling hairless bulldogs who taunted each other by pointing proudly to their abdominal regions. The young woman Mariko prepared to meet in the ring had the bone structure of a mailbox, all steely, round edges. Alkie and I waited with Mariko in the locker room. She held her head between her legs and had already thrown up twice.

"Go check again for me, okay?"

Mariko wanted Alkie to check the stands for her parents. He'd looked four times before, and from the sound of Mariko's voice this would be the last time. Each time Alkie returned without saying anything, which was clear to us all. While Alkie was away, Mariko came over and sat next to me, close enough for our arms and thighs to touch. Her hands were tucked into those gloves like two puffed mangoes, and her shampoo smelled sweeter than I'd ever noticed. She looked like a woman already defeated. We had only two things to say to each other. Two promises to make.

"I think Alkie likes you," she told me.

"I want your name on our submission," I told her.

It was done. If possible I would have fought for Mariko in the ring as well with mango fists. In that moment she didn't seem to care about the impending bodily harm she would soon endure. Her fighting skills had not improved since the first day she walked into class with a swollen lip and all the possibilities on earth. She would lose that fight and win the physics prize. Her family attended the award ceremony, and I took a photo of them. Alkie and I would never see the beating in the ring that night because she told us to stay in the locker room. He asked me what I was thinking, and I told him blueberry pancakes. He smiled and the pink of his gums made me giggle a feeling that spread fast and hard from my cheeks to tailbone like paint thrown on a canvas. Alkie hovered over me and pushed my shoulders down onto the bench. The harsh fluorescent lights fluttered like a hundred hummingbirds. He pressed hard against my ribs and navel, pulling my upper lip with both of his. We made our exchange, Mariko and I, two lives borrowed for as long as possible. Alkie kissed me with such familiarity that I knew I'd lost myself, every memory only dreamed and time rewound to another life unequal in scope and imagination, one of frayed liquid ropes that brush every atom of the universe.

A BRIEF EXCERPT FROM
THE HISTORY OF SALT

Woman of the silver minivan approached the store with her three small children as passengers. There was a rip in her sweatpants and a chocolate stain on her breast, but that was all right. She wasn't going to leave the minivan. Her eldest son in whom there was no confidence would do the shopping. Woman of the silver minivan desired only one item, one crucial thing. "Buy salt," she told her eldest son in whom she had no confidence. Their eyes met, and he warmed with the desire to do well, to prove to her that the previous seven years of his life amounted to more than a blinding white heap of tiny disappointments. There were the other two children who sat in wait, but the woman of the silver minivan knew better than to send them. There was the youngest boy who was thought to have lived. He fell into the swimming pool of their backyard for nine seconds when he was four years old. His ghost sank to the bottom as his body was scooped up from above; they've been bored without each other ever since. The eldest girl, not quite worth mentioning, has never been able to disagree. With the personality of a candy dispenser, she will give all she has if you tilt her head and will grow to please many men. The boy in whom there was no confidence smiled at the woman of the silver minivan. Her right ear twitched, telling him this is the last time. "Buy salt," she said, "the kind with the little girl on it," and handed him money. So he left the car to purchase the salt, the salt with the label that had a little girl walking in the rain. Two old men in blue vests guarded the entrance to the store like gargoyles with shopping carts. They spewed greetings and smiles to the shoppers but gave none to the boy because he was small and less than handsome. The boy in whom there was no confidence was not deterred. He knew what he wanted, the box of salt with the little girl on it, he thought. She wore a raincoat, held an open umbrella, and stepped prettily to nowhere at all. The boy in whom there was no confidence moved swiftly through the aisles, stopping only to lift a pineapple he could not resist. Then he saw her, the little girl on the carton of salt, and he put her under his arm. The boy waited in line, his money dampening in his palm. He was terribly close to proving himself quite capable when all went wrong. He turned his head for reasons unknown and there stood an unremarkable sight to nearly all, including her mother. A little girl with the worst luck in the world held a plastic umbrella hooked to her elbow. She held the umbrella open and dragged it on the floor, hoping the store's fluorescent lights would burst into a trickle of electric rain. She had only one shoe and a dirty flat foot with green nails on pretty, brown toes. And so the boy in whom there was no confidence forgot his salt, forgot the woman, and forgot her silver minivan. He followed that girl and her terrible luck until she finally stopped and noticed. She noticed he was small, not quite handsome, rather incompetent, and that was all she ever expected. They shared a long life and died together in bed, sleeping as they had for thousands of nights. On that last night they lay breathing deeply, then slowly as the grain of each breath grew finer and finer. Cool white gusts of carbonated air crushed together above their heads as each exhaled happily into nothing at all.

EPHEMEROS

He comes out fast, rights his body for the big reveal, gives a kick off like launching a bobsled, upside down to the world, hoping his mother would appreciate the help, hoping she might not miss him too much. He lies on his back supine to the soft nursery light while his legs grow thicker then longer, and his torso matches the mad dash into adolescence, the crib aching and crumpling beneath before he spills off completely like a pumpkin from the bed of toy truck. He has to urinate, so he goes, on purpose in that spot, for them to think on. Soon he can walk, has big bones, and the memories of yesterdays come back to him: the words, all the words for meat and milk and sex plus the need for them all. He staggers to the mental ward because they understand how to clothe a man who is wet and naked and ask few questions as possible. He is four hours old and no one cares. He meets his first friend and tells him the story of how he lives a life in a single day and night. The friend is blind and a fellow patient and believes him. The friend suggests he spend his day eating a bunch of cookies, meaning cocaine or hookers or somebody you really love. He tells him he does not know anyone to love yet and certainly would not eat them, but it was almost sunrise and therefore getting late, so he left the hospital. Without food or love, he was left with anger and began to knock over parts of the world, a branch, a café table, a teenager, and as he struggled to pull down a yield sign, swing it out of its concrete and mud socket, shouts of a protest crept up. Before he could leave to rage in quiet, he notices her, mouth wide and chanting with a paper banner across her chest. It is almost noon, and there is gray in his beard and less hair on his head. The sun is high, and he is too old for her, but picks up the loose end of her banner and chants along. There are others who rage nearby and want to do more than scream, and then they do. There is fire and gas grenades and police batons and handcuffs, but he pulls her away to hide and wait it out. She tells him she hoped for peace. He tells her that he'd never seen that and only hoped for a sandwich and a wife. She tells him about her car. They spend the afternoon in the car where he finds his love and his meat, and together they watch the smoke rise from burning stores and listen for the chatter of every other person about invisible myths that govern them. She falls asleep, and he feels the arthritic impulse to rest with her but knows he cannot. He remembers vaguely a friend he knew and wanders back during visiting hours at the hospital. The friend is having pudding and offers some and asks about the day he's had. He doesn't remember much but tells his friend one thing that is so clear, being born the first time a very long time ago, a hard birth like wringing oil from a peach pit because he was afraid to leave and sorry for his mother. Tomorrow he will try something different, tuck in deep and roll out smooth, cannonball-style.

DOG PEOPLE

My lover wants to eat me, I'm sure. I don't know if I met her as a man or something else; I've been so many things for her since. One afternoon she gave me that look that says you don't have to do it if you don't want to, but I know you will because I know you. So there I was, on her lap, big as a pillow with round eyes and a heartbeat, hypoallergenic. I can hardly bear the great and terrible vicissitudes of life as a dog. When she leaves for work, the emptiness of the apartment becomes so dense and absolute that I cry for an hour at the door. Resentment tingles in my gums, and I have to chew. I chew for us. When we play together, all the world is light in the chase of her, away and back, away and back. I hoped always that it didn't end, but she ended it always.

When we cook, I am a translucent, old woman, a faint likeness of the mother she buried. She used to ask me things, such as what is death like and why did I have to die? I help her on holidays with big complicated roasts and pies. I remind her that death isn't so bad. She reminds me life is hard. We fight over spices. The light that passes through me is beautiful, darkened slightly as if swallowed by every manner of devotion. She thinks she's inheriting my bunions. I tell her to be kinder to her father.

On Saturday afternoons we go to the mall in wedge sandals, too much makeup, and almost no money. We might try on cheap jewelry. Once I stole a necklace for her. At home I gave her the loot, and she was disappointed. She said that she forgot I did things like that when she was a child. I reminded her that she was my best friend and said we should practice kissing. She laughed, and we were all right again. She asked, if you were a pear and I took a bite, would that hurt? My God, yes, I said. She wished I could meet her dog and boyfriend. It was my turn to laugh.

On days that we make love it is a constant thing. I tell her we should pace ourselves or she will not want to see me this way for another week. She doesn't care, and I may spend the next three days as a dog. Being a man seems a very sensible thing to be. When most breathless, she tells me I am a miracle. I wish the impossible wish, to keep her there.

In order to love her just one way, I have to be the love she has known in every other direction. There is one possible thing in the midst of our uneven lives. In this manner, we can be together as nothing else can. I will wait for her on the foot of our bed. I will be in season, Bartlett, the best of pears. She will eye my sweet meat, and the last light will pass over the horizon of her tongue as I am sewn into my love one bite at a time.

BARBERS

When a girl is raised by an elderly aunt and a rogue father, there are many needs that have to be met. First came the need to do my brother's hair, so we wouldn't look poor. I brushed it backward for the first two years then learned that forward was best when it had been cut close. I used electric clippers on the hairline to make it ruler perfect. There were days he should have been photographed and put on barbershop walls for inspiration. He needed to sit still as concrete for that to happen. He needed to grip a toy car in his palm tight because to drop it would disturb his sister's concentration, and he might have had to go to school with a patch missing from the back again. During those years there came the need to manage my breasts and teeth: wire for both when money came. After too many decades of pork rinds and fried catfish consumption there came the need for Aunt Arlene to die. It happened two months after my nineteenth birthday. College remained the only option. In college I found a roommate, a beautiful Filipina who cheated on her boyfriend with men and women. The boyfriend had narrow shoulders, lovely lips and said to call him Lou. I borrowed Lou for the thrill and kept him when the roommate said, "I don't give a hot fuck." Lou was a freegan and taught me how not to just endure but thrive without money. Together we scavenged Dumpsters for food and décor. He said things like "you can't really tell people about this" or "my own family wouldn't get it" or "don't we look like cousins" or "I wish I looked as good as you without makeup." Early on, sex between us happened out of instinct and protocol like holding a door open for a stranger. Soon we were not strange to one another. I wore his deodorant, and he wore my eyeliner. We did nude yoga while my roommate ate agave pumpkin muffins on the balcony per her gluten-free diet. On a particular afternoon Lou removed my underwear and put them on. He asked to be rubbed through the fabric. Soon after that, we stopped touching altogether. Lou said, "I'm going to become a woman. In Thailand. It's cheaper. They're good though." I went too. Not only were the genitals reconfigured and hormones indulged, but the face as well. They shaved the skull and jaw to feminine lines. He lay on the operating room table with much of his face on a tray while the surgeon leaned over and removed the stubble of bone one measured thrust at a time. In the delirium of painkillers I told my boyfriend (now girlfriend) that I was in love with her. She replied, "You aren't queer, just ambivalent." I wanted to slap her new face but slipped in the silence and pretended I, too, could be made over, neat again.

END OF THE WORLD

Surprise, Arizona, just another dig-a-hole suburb of Phoenix is where Carl inherited his home, right up against the state park, leading to the White Tank mountains so no developer could spring up a row of houses to block his view while he waited for the big thing. Mountains weren't necessarily good except to look at; they might be hard to get into, get over, get out of, or get around if the big thing forced him out of the house and to another bug-out spot. Carl worked in the lighting section of the big-box home improvement store twelve minutes away, lucky, not like most of his neighbors who commute an hour and ten minutes each way into downtown Phoenix, or worse, Tempe or Scottsdale for work. *Failure to add water to the fill-line may cause product to ignite,* the instructions on his noodle bowl for lunch, a food product that may violently combust during preparation, usually served as Carl's only theater; that and the clientele from the lingerie thrift shop across the street.

Lady D walked in to his department carrying a hunk of glass and wire that looked like it had been surgically removed from a mechanical dragon, and Carl knew the big thing arrived. Lady D owned the thrift shop. Both the lingerie and the owner tumbled recklessly out of a nineteenth-century brothel full of women the same height and weight of a modern seven-year-old. Kentucky Fried Chicken is to blame for the massive bone enlargement of the contemporary human, not Lady D, though, since she had the diminutive frame of centuries-dead whores, plus the lace and the scentless leather. Old leather doesn't smell like the new stuff. Retail is like war, long stretches of boredom punctuated by brief moments of panic. No chaotic grace breathed in that store, every wall punched with a lone bloom of light in an order too contrived to exist in nature. The linear rows of CFLs dotted out from right angles and emptied the aisle of any beauty the overwhelming wash of energy might have.

The big thing could happen once a year or twice in one week. A raging team of pee-wee football players could pour in and just smash the place to hell, bang their tiny helmets on the shelves, bust the lightbulbs with their teeth, cast their bodies around like the whole store was an enormous microwave and they were radiation pounding atom upon atom. Maybe the team carried the zombie virus, and Carl would be obliged to eradicate them all. That's when the big thing turns into an ethical dilemma. Carl spent his spare time, which was all of his time, preparing for the big things. He stored water in clusters of plastic jugs around the job and, of course, at home and in his car, plus the tactical packs, bug-out bags, and all the essentials: fixed blade knife, folding shovel, rope, gas mask, water purification tablets, military grade MREs that tasted like coyote shit, ibuprofen, Tylenol, anti-acids, Neosporin, salt, canned chili peppers, peanut butter, flares, tinfoil, sewing kit, ChapStick, deck of cards in case he gets bored after the big thing, and socks (lots of socks). His emergency kits came in a variety of sizes, and whether he had enough was a question Carl could not answer.

Diedre, Diane, Diana, Delores, Deborah. Lady D owned all of the salacious names for women and not girls. Modeling her store's wares was a hobby and good marketing strategy. The worst outfit for nuclear fallout might be Lady D's whalebone corset, fishnet stockings and purple satin gloves. She put her shapeless glass/wire creation on the counter for Carl. Your shit product fried my lamp, she said. All around the two of them burned a few hundred lights, some on strings, most just plugged into the walls like a psychotic garden. Lady D spoke to Carl with a tone somewhere in between patience and fury like she couldn't decide if he had Asperger's or was just an asshole. Through the window, Carl watched an unusually tall couple enter Lady D's shop. Vikings. Threats. Homosexuals. Vegetarians. In his world every kind of other person was a sadistic twelve-year-old with a BB gun, and he remained the world's only plump pigeon. Carl did not yet have the nerve to resist the will of someone else, especially an upset customer, and especially an old woman in a bustier. He prepared to give her everything she wanted, including a new power cord for her ancient lamp, a full refund, store credit and his soul if she demanded.

Though she visited Carl's store regularly, Carl never once entered Lady D's lingerie shop. He knew how the experience would turn out for him. He goes into the shop, takes it all in, the stockings on mannequin legs, the ones that look like nets he could cut open and maybe make useful, women buying panties from the rows of them in every color too bright for camouflage, useless for anything but a distress rag, so he bypasses all of it and buys something safe, something more complimentary and barely for sale, gum he selects from the gumball machine in the corner and puts twenty dollars on the counter for change where the cashier, prettier than Carl is allowed to look on directly, waits for him to put something else on the counter, too, but all he has is the bill, the fruity sweetness of the gum fragrant through the container; it becomes stressful, the waiting for the cashier to realize this is all he wants to buy, but she does realize and says she has no change at the moment, has to get it from the back of the store, all the while a line forms, indicating Carl should give it up, retreat, but she tells him to stay, holds him with a hand out in the air above his heart and calls to Lady D in the quiet hidden rooms all stores have, counting inventory, shouting back orders to the cashier in irritated tones, orders to just buy the damn gum for him, and she'll pay her back if she looks through her purse for change, which she does as Carl goes to leave, but the hand raises again, stills him in the presence of a little girl appearing at his side that has seen more R-rated movies than Carl, the ones with violence and no sex or cursing, just exploding heads and alien entrails and white guts and brain matter because that must not be as bad as saying fuck or doing that word, according to the rating system, who with ease buys a gumball, slips the coin in, activates the shoot where the gum rolls out of the metal door into her tiny hand, payday, enjoys it, teeth like a car compactor in a junkyard, sweet crush, and buys another to pocket, for later among customers behind Carl, frozen as he is, unable to break through Carl's embarrassment and give him a quarter because that would make all the previous waiting for his own solution invalid, and a decent human can't do that to another without causing some kind of damage. He dared not make the discomfort of his imagination, the horror of a memory.

Carl hated some people but not all people, just enough to collapse reality and cling to the hope that one day he will have an excuse to shoot the ears off anyone who tried to steal his stockpile of dried apricots. The world he was promised as a child never manifested. Good, clean boys didn't always win the prize. But if every country, city, or parish boiled back down to its marrow, basic survival would be all that was left. Carl would be king. That kept him awake, organizing his materials, routing his evasive plans to get out of the city off main roads; that and his love of Lady D, along with wondering when the exact point children stop being people if the apocalypse occurred. When do their rights dissolve, and it is no longer an adult's unspoken obligation to protect them?

Lady D cursed at Carl for taking too long with her lamp. She accused him of filling his days with Pop-Tarts and orange jelly beans, declared him useless to the world in a way that was unfair to the people who loved him—the people he partitioned off from when they refused to understand. He consciously condemned himself to a hermetic existence, pulled the fluorescent shell of light around his tender fat and muscle, and reveled in the right to slobbery. Then in a quiet pulse the room darkened: power outage. Without windows in the huge warehouse total darkness swamped the aisles; Carl felt the big thing had happened, knew exactly what to do, how to save Lady D and a few of her employees if she wanted, the smartest most loyal of them, while the rest fluttered off like gnats to be pressed under the thumb of a new world order. They stood together, Carl and Lady D, two shadows not much different in depth or height, paired by gentle circumstances, a quiet stop to a loud and unkind universe. Their union lasted only for a few seconds before the power was restored in a sudden, violent tide that blew out several wall accessories, and Carl stood in the beating core of a new civilization, post big thing, about to continue where he left off.

WAYS TO MOURN AN ASSHOLE

Once is not enough. Believe in Santa and Jesus and Clark and Bruce but only 'til daylight. Remember not to be a child. Pretend to be ill. Wear black slacks. Pray. Cut your hair without a mirror. Buy a casket. Use the casket. Invite all of the friends. Invite no one at all. Bury the empty casket. Collect the ashes. Hold the ashes. Kick the ashes with your heel. Be glad the plastic did not break. Put the ashes away for later. Play basketball. Write an obituary. Remember not to be small. Go hunting. Go mountain climbing. Remember to be very strong. Look at your muscles. Touch your abs. Remember to be proud. Take out the death certificates. Make copies of the death certificates. Draw penises on the back of the copies. Draw faces on the penises. Put the originals away for the insurance company. Open the ashes. Smell the ashes. Cough. Feel a little sick and shake it off. Put the ashes in glass containers. Pretend they are Canopic jars. Pretend to be a pharaoh. Pretend these are the organs of ancestors. Pretend to come from greatness. Remember not to be afraid. Put one jar outside for the rain. Kill ants outside with an index finger while the rain falls. Remember to be big. Go inside. Open the plastic bag from the hospital full of clothes. Take out the wallet. Pocket a hundred and sixty-eight dollars. Look at the driver's license. Pull out the belt. Wear the belt. Remember to get fat enough to fit the belt. Collect the jar of wet ashes. Drop the license inside. Take the license out and wipe it off. Put the jar of ashes and rain in the freezer. Take it out of the freezer the next day. Sit it out on the fence. Find your hunting rifle. Fire one shot. Miss. Fire again. Don't miss. Remember not to care. Remember there are other jars left.

RITES

We formed a coven in the fall. Lynwood, California. Fall didn't have the romance or the chill of Salem like we had in our heads, but it was eighth grade. We always had sanctuary at Marisol's house. Things got real when the praying mantis showed up. Her yard was more deep than wide, encased in a cinder block fence, all grass except for a shade tree with a name I didn't know, but it had leaves that knew when to change color, when to fall off, and when to grow back, so it seemed a good spot. Every single one of us had some degree of effed-up-ness. Our tiny charter school prided itself on addressing the "total student." So we wound up in Partners for Progress. Beware all alliteration; when it comes to school programs it means somebody stupid stitched this shit up. The classroom we met in had cold chairs, fake pumpkins and cornucopias, all plastic. Real light came in through just one window, frosted over by age and carbon dioxide from the procession of a thousand mouth-breathers over decades. The whole thing was just detention for lashing out in nonviolent ways. The four of us lacked social skills, understatement of the millennium. We had no friends, but for a while we had each other. The real problem was we had no vision, at least not their vision of our futures, our destinies, our careers in medicine, accounting, or retail stumbled upon out of necessity more than ambition. We were supposed to go on to have intermittent tragedies, teeny tiny and ginormous among the usual swath of nothing but regular life, including marriage, disease, and babies that were cute from ages thirteen months to four years and not so much after. I was the worst but never said it out loud, even to my earth sisters. Danielle, Marisol, Sherry, and I were broken and weren't going to be set free until we got it, absorbed the destiny everybody else wanted for us. We had to figure out how to get what they wanted us to have on our terms.

We were convening in Marisol's backyard when Sherry brought the mantis over. She had it in a sandwich bag, which was stupid, so Marisol gave her a mason jar that was still full of watermelon rind preserves that her mom didn't want. We made a circle of ourselves in the grass out back and poured the contents of the jar into the center.

We also didn't like reading, so we got most of our research about witches from *Buffy* episodes. Couldn't tell belladonna from red pepper flakes, and it didn't matter. The fake magic was just a reason to be together. Being together is what gave us power. Anytime three or more women join up for the same reason and come to complete agreement, a hell mouth opens up somewhere far off. It opens up, and some tortured soul either escapes or is invited. I don't have proof, but it does that some place with so few people that anybody who sees it would just be dismissed as a crazy mountain dweller who wears squirrel underwear and eats berries straight from bushes. Somewhere like Montana. None of us looked like the TV-pretty actresses that play the outcasts. Marisol had shark mouth. Rows and rows of teeth just crowded in there like a rave, except without the sex. Her mom was tormented by it, dental bills up the rear. She looked at Marisol like she was a puzzle all the time. Still, her mom made us toast and jelly whenever we were over, so she was cool even if she judged her own daughter unfairly, condemning her ugliness, fighting it with needles and wire and surgery and Novocain like it was her fault so she would fix it at all cost, pain being the price. Danielle hated her extra hundred pounds and would never really eat in front of us. She posted depressing tweets: Can't go bowling, so go Velveeta #foreveralone #fatgirlproblems. We didn't talk about it, just got her drunk on triple sec every once in a while so she would look happy. Sherry looked like her dad, which was unfortunate. She had the biggest boobs out of all of us with a man's forehead and nose. Pointless, to say the least. I just stared at her boobs to be safe most of the time, to feel something. I wasn't all gay for her because she wasn't smart enough to like the full way at all. It would've been silly, like being gay for a large-chested seahorse.

A whiff of sweet rot escaped that suggested Marisol's mom didn't seal that lid properly. Cinnamon, cloves, water, salt, and white sugar all ran into an oily pool at the heart of our circle—iridescent sheen like webbing still in liquid form, warm in the spider's bulb. I wanted to set it on fire. Danielle wondered whether the rinds were any good #wastenotwantnot.

Before the killings, whenever we gathered together we watched TV and put our bare feet in the naked ground at least once each. *Bizarre Foods* was a favorite. The main guy goes around eating weird shit from weird places and loving it like crazy. He made us all want to feel scorpion on our tongues or whale blubber salad. One time he was on a boat, scooped a pregnant fish out of the ocean, slit open her belly to let the fetal babies fall out, picked one up, and bit its head off. The way he chewed the unborn fish skull, robbed it of its womb like a god, and described the taste as fresh like seawater; it was hot, and I knew I had problems.

Sherry rinsed the jar out and shook the mantis inside. It had a green brighter than should be possible and was unbearably pretty, red eyes and all. Then she asked how we should do it, *it* being murder. That's when Danielle pitched a fit and begged us not to. We looked at her, and she burst into flames, flames meaning tears, knowing that she wasn't supposed to disagree. Dissent was the enemy among all else. Soon she got a hold of herself and calmed down. The unhappy resolve to kill settled in her brows, and we moved on. Marisol thought we were supposed to make wishes before killing, but that seemed wrong. Wishes were meant for things eternal like the stars or angels or good love songs. Wishes meant you were asking and not taking. We were taking, and we all wanted very specific things. The tiny green life in the jar belonged to us. Something extraordinary could have happened, something so daring and glorious that even if we died doing it, the world would've been like that was crazy and great and what a loss to not have those four around anymore. I learned a lot about the cost of things. What we wanted, whole normal lives would cost something heavy. We paid the price and got good at it. Death is subjective on occasion. Like anybody, we started small and ended big: burned some ants, tried to hit birds with rocks, but no athlete existed among us. We had to be smart: poison in the seed. Danielle cried a lot then, and we spent most of the time convincing each other that this is what we did; this is what our power was all about. Beauty was stupid and easy and didn't provide anything useful. Our demands had to be more than that. They had to be for each other and not ourselves to work, but we hadn't figured that out yet. Our power was staying close, closer than blood would allow, aware of each other's essence down to the marmalade crusted on our cuticles. Human sacrifice was the end goal from the beginning. We all knew that. It was important to know, even if no one said it.

Sherry drowned the mantis before we'd had time to sit with our thoughts. I chopped her in the throat for acting too soon. Danielle started to cry again, and the whole afternoon turned to shit. And that wasn't all. Our school didn't see enough progress in our partnership anyway. We showed up to the room; it smelled like nothing alive not even dust, just oils from plastics and disinfectant. We sat under the fogged-up window like posed, lunatic Barbies. Danielle still showed up, shirt collar damp with throw up from a weak attempt at an eating disorder. Hoarder of stolen cosmetics, Sherry, slouched arms folded under boobs, her backpack loaded with compacts and eyeliners (all the wrong shades) from unattended purses. Tic-tac-toe boards etched into Marisol's thighs were no well-kept secrets. The school wanted to try something different. They were going to break us up, put us with individual counselors every evening instead. Our sanctuary would become artificial. We would have no reason to be together anymore, and we would never be whole if that happened. The hour to make it all worthwhile had to come soon.

Because we never learned to do any research or read anything at all ever, we quickly made up our own rules of the coven. We had to kill something again to make up for the wasted mantis in a jar disaster. The other rule was that we had to do it with our minds. Pick the prey without saying so aloud, and if we all thought about the same victim, death would come. We were sure of it. When Sherry's cousin's dog died, we got excited. We knew it was a fluke and couldn't take credit, but we were closing in. Emergency vehicles showed up at Marisol's neighbor's house, and our hopes swelled. But it was just a lady that chewed on her pearl necklace out of habit and one day sucked down a bead. Her son made the call. She lived.

Then the last rule finally occurred to us. We could change something about our sisters but nothing about ourselves. If we picked something for ourselves, we'd pick something superficial, something too easy that would make us weaker in the long run. Like Sherry, if she wished, she'd wish herself free of her father's expression and be left with nothing but extraordinary breasts. A girl like that, weak-willed like Sherry, would just end up hooked on oxy with nothing to look forward to except the next amateur porn clip she could post online.

Self-reflection is a blind spot. Even then we knew that much. The four of us sat cross-legged around the sticky ant pile that used to be candied watermelon, held hands, and hummed a little bit for the drama of it. The genetic imprints of malice and misfortune could be smoothed away like wrinkles in plastic wrap. Sherry had her father's face and his temperament and his propensity for addiction and his impulsiveness. Danielle was easier. If big girls eat their feelings, Danielle was a glutton for loneliness. If we did nothing, Marisol would go on to hate herself because her mother taught her how, one bitter gaze at a time. I had to trust that my sisters knew what to fix about me. We were going to make it all better. Someone just had to die for it to happen. We finally got it. Death would give us the lives we were supposed to have, the lives according to school, to the state of California, to the whole wide world. We reconvened, concentrated again, ignored the cold under the shade tree. The wet grass felt like home. We dug deep; we dug hard; we dug long, both feet in the ground. My toenails carved up the roots. At the end we knew we'd done it.

A little girl. She was too young and too talented for us to know personally, but we knew of her. She died the way healthy kids always die, hung up in blinds maybe or a pool unattended. She was the kind of girl that would have been popular, not because of her tits and teeth but her generosity and dirty jokes. She would've grown up long-limbed and capable, played the bass guitar in band and accordion for fun. She would've watched spaghetti westerns with her grandpa at Christmas and always have done the dishes. Everyone would've had a crush on her and felt it reciprocated but not in the creepy way that ends in a felony and a lifetime of psychotherapy. In her twenties she would've developed an online gambling habit that crushed her mother's heart and savings. Later a catering business with an apple theme would generate enough funds to pay off her debt and send her mom and dad on a cruise the spring before her father passes. She would've married twice, once happily and adopted after losing her first child in a miscarriage. She would have loved and been loved easy like a mint, when gone no one would be left tormented because the pleasure is understood to be intense and temporary. That's the life we believe we had taken. Later on, I heard Danielle confessed. She would. They put her in therapy for weeks and convinced her we had nothing to do with it, of course. We disbanded our coven. We made different friends by summer, ones that often disagreed with us. We adopted their dream. We could see it out in front of us, waiting clear as the sun going up and down, over and over. We seemed just fine. We were just fine. We all went on to live safe, ordinary lives.

THEY ONLY LOOK LIKE
THEY'RE SMILING

Blabbermouth Vicki caught me talking to the turtle tank in the break room. Now everybody knows and is making a big deal out of my days as an animal physiotherapist. We're all trying to save something here. No one works at a not-for-profit out of total selfishness, just mostly selfishness. I don't even know what or whom we're trying to save anymore, victims of natural disasters, ostriches with mange, that same boy they've been showing on TV commercials for twenty years crying with a fly in the corner of his eye, or cats with gimp paws. I shrug. They're all in the pool of great and awful pity, and we're all at the edges cheering them on, filling the pool to the brim with our tears and palm sweat. It gives us purpose. The only thing I like about Vicki is that she gets it. I hate just about everything else. She happens to have diarrhea of the mouth, so I can't talk to her about anything at all and not feel like I just cc'd the entire office. It was Vicki's whole effing idea to do a company trip to the marine park, which we had to pay for out of pocket, including transportation/ lodging. It ended the way it always ended. Everyone nose-dived into the nearest bottle of liquor and turned into a gaggle of gushy, violent, fornicating adolescents.

There is one person who understands why I talk to the turtle. Erika smells good like a baby's head, so she never goes on dates or anything because people just want to protect her and ask her how she's doing or bring her juice but not actually get close to her that way. She knows it. Sometimes she wears this ode de geriatric femme perfume that makes her look shorter and weak wristed, but the baby aroma comes through just fine still. I think she hopes mixing her scent with an old woman will balance things off, but uh-uh. Erika is in love with Caleb who is in love with Anne who is our boss and has expressions that say *oh no she didn't* but knuckles that look like they've made a few grown men brush lips with the concrete, so we all love Anne for hiring mostly women to work in an organization that probably helps struggling women in this country or another with microloans, quite possibly, but I am no longer sure. Caleb and I never talk because we aren't the same kind of people, and we are both jealous over Erika because she's our favorite little sister even though she is three years older than I am with different parents. We both want her to get her big girl teeth and go to college and stay away from bad boys who don't do anything bad other than abuse the women that dare to love them, which is pretty bad. Caleb and I know what kind of anal debris can waddle in a room and steal her heart, so we both fight in silence over who has more power over Erika's future.

The turtle speaks to me too. We don't have names for each other because that's not what turtles are into. We know each other because we look right at each other. I can talk to other animals that live in water, something about the flow of liquid over our voices, the tendrils in my ears. I don't know what the fuck it is, but we can do it. Years ago I used to be bullied for it, but times they are a-changing. So, it's something I talk about when I have to. Vicki makes sure I have to. Caleb is all tight cheeked because of the dolphin incident at the marine park. We still fight quietly, without words or gestures, with one another over Erika, but I was winning for a while because I wasn't raped by a dolphin in front of the entire office. And if I were, I'm sure I would have the wherewithal to recognize it and not look absolutely gleeful during the entire experience. I told the turtle about it, and he/she just couldn't believe it. I didn't know how to explain what a dolphin was without showing a picture, but the picture on my phone was really small so the whole being assaulted by something that could fit in a human's hand seemed too baffling, so instead we talked about how the microwaved food—bologna sandwiches, fast food chili, gyros and Mountain Dew in the break room made the turtle tank water funky day in and day out. We all blamed the smell of the break room on the actual turtle tank, but I didn't say that because I thought it might be offensive.

Effing Vicki brought rum. At the hotel she confessed in the lobby that she thought nobody liked her then threw up. The whole trip felt like punching yourself in the face. I purchased a churro for Erika before Caleb even thought of it. She didn't like the strawberry filling (who would?), so I ate the rest of hers, even the parts that she put her tiny teeth on, because I had to teach her not to be wasteful. Vicki insisted we had to buy tickets to the private dolphin pool before we even got to the park as part of the company package. I read on the brochure that it was optional and therefore shit-filled Vicki struck again. Still, private pool happened. The rest involved dolphin rape, not rape of dolphins, which would be heinous and should be left in old wives' tales of seventeenth-century pirates on long voyages that ended in scurvy/starvation/hallucination/marine bestiality. This was modern-day vengeance of the porpoise because it is about power after all. They only look like they're smiling, Jesse, the trainer, told us. Jesse looked as if she hadn't smiled in a long time. I began inventing reasons for her very obvious unhappiness. She had a chlorine-washed ponytail probably soaked in odorless sea animal saliva, which in most situations is far from sexy. Still, she didn't give off the sex is my problem kind of vibe (too little or too much). I figured Jesse had just the right combination of no sex or a big fat vat of it, so instead the misery had to be corporate in origin. Anne sent us all a group text that we made fun of, but we replied to immediately acknowledging her busy schedule as a legitimate reason for missing the company outing. That's when Kitka the bottle-nose went to town on Caleb. He'd been stroking the belly as men are instructed to do by Jesse and gave Kitka a big bear hug in the pool. Kitka didn't dislodge from that hug for several seconds and tossed Caleb around a bit in the water. The entire event seemed pretty obvious to everyone but Caleb. Even Jesse blew her whistle furiously, which made my ears ache something terrible. Caleb looked so happy. Vicki nearly passed out from joy.

After watching the tape on YouTube, Caleb sent me a hostile email accusing me of siccing the dolphin on him, which never occurred to me. The dolphin said some things, but they talk really fast. I just heard things like jingle, jingle and potato chip, potato chip, potato chip and all the usual manic clicking that adds up to the same thing as *um* or *like* or *I just meant* or *even so* or *huh* or *one more* in human speak. I never talked to Kitka, didn't even let on that I could because it doesn't seem wise to go around chatting up every sea creature with a brain. They're kind of like us in that they have their ways and such. The thing that I didn't expect to happen (even though that dolphin bit shocked a little) was Erika and her crush on me now. The churro eating probably did it, but I can't tell her that liking me like that is wrong and against nature somehow without saying being near her makes me think of Saturday morning cartoons and Winnie the Pooh paraphernalia of every kind. Instead, I avoid her except for texts, which I keep brief, and use the safest of emojis like fists and beer mugs and laughing monkeys to show her what to stay away from and maybe associate that with myself as a wall of protection now that I know soft, sensitive types like me are Erika's choice and not wobbly footed anuses with hooker on their partner's sex resume. So, in the end, Caleb did all the winning; took all my glory with Erika. They spend their time talking face to face the way we used to while I text her ninja turtles that laugh and wiggling sperm whales then wait for her to look down at her phone and feel something pure about me.

There she stood all wrecked from the inside out, not that her clothes or hair or anything fell out of order, just the internal tendons of her soul appeared frayed. Old jump rope. Vicki could be different if she tried, if she talked like a good human or even the no-nonsense way of the turtle. She could be my Erica, one with a grown-woman smell of detergent and fertility, not the clean, woodsy perfume that grows inside new Barbie doll boxes. I wanted to do something sudden and violent to Vicki like propose marriage. The want of her made me resent her, the clumsy execution of managerial duties made me resent her, and the way she always appeared eaten. And yes, she did appear eaten. Something weary and dreadful like her own body had consumed her. I realized she continuously flopped around as if she were a regurgitated, soggy clog coughed up from her own throat; the cause and effect of bad choices. But she saw me, wanted to speak to and hear me in ways I preserved for everyone else. An intensity that suggested all kinds of contradictions breached the membranes of my awareness: runaway devotion. Vicki presented herself in the doorway, a mammoth peanut, uncooked. I prophesied our future together, her smooth surface coated in a layer of residual moisture from countless lickings over every exposed molecule, unsanitary as the Blarney stone and just as full of delightful, arduous destiny.

THE IMMOLATOR

In protest of unyielding circumstances, monks have been known to walk into public squares and quietly set themselves on fire. I prefer to make noise. I bake bread now and die a little every day in flour and yeast. He says pumpernickel over my shoulder, and I want to vomit. That is my husband, and he is the kind of happy that makes you dizzy just to be around. His joy is my paint thinner and will probably kill me. He still has those big, bulging eyes like something cold-blooded and scaly, but he really is pretty and nothing but ordinary. When we dated decades ago, I told him I could do something special. I could get really, really hot. Of course, the guys loved that line right up until I turned a clod of sand to glass in my palm. Most tried to seem unimpressed, but it is intimidating. So most didn't call again. Eventually I met someone not afraid; we all do. As a young woman I lived. At least I can say it, even in the past tense. It used to be fun, before, looking for trouble. I'm slew-footed with narrow shoulders—from far away a victim through and through. I wandered the world alone at night just to see what might happen, just to dare someone to come closer. Will is a terrible thing. The night is full of people who want things and have no will to resist the yearning. It climbs on the brain and makes wicked roots that wind down to prick every tender muscle that needs nothing but rest. I only maimed only a few scumbags by happenchance. Lots just pulled up in their cars and wanted service by the half hour. I soldered their doors shut with a finger and lectured them on the symptoms of chlamydia. Then they sped off. I learned all of the different words for vagina back then. That was high school. I lost my appetite for scumbags in my twenties and thirties. Although I almost joined one of those teams. They all have embarrassing names with animals or adjectives (Elkman, The Cicada, or Mr. Indelible), but I call them dash men because they dash. They dash off buildings to save the suicidal or the clumsy. They dash out of cars to stop hungry editorial assistants from mugging their neighbors. They dash between school buses and train cars and between disinterested parents and ungrateful children. They dash in between the sheets of cute, vapid twenty-somethings who wonder what it's like to blow a superhero. Each dash man is unique as the dash symbol (–), a placeholder, anything more exciting at a glance than an ordinary man. The dash men and their teams of extraordinary people aim to avenge injustice or some shit and always try to recruit me.

Everyone goes through a charitable stage. That kind of selfless giving certainly must be good for us—to build houses in the third world, pass out blankets and water to victims of natural disasters, collect toys for children at Christmas. It was my husband's idea to join. He went to the first meeting with me at the YMCA. They had two fliers, a strong old lady, and a little girl that moved too fast to see. The girl kept untying people's shoes. One of the fliers in jeans and a blazer glided over the group with a plate of sugar cookies and offered us a couple. He said this was the only group for nonordinary citizens within two hundred miles. They stayed involved in the community and went on "missions." The team's latest mission resulted in an animal shelter evacuation from a carbon monoxide leak. The inside giggles were hard to suppress. You could help, he said. The flier was right, but I didn't commit because their cookies lacked salt. When we were finally back outside, I laughed harder than I had in years. "At least they don't wear costumes." My husband stopped in the street and looked at me with his incredulous gecko face. "I thought you would love it. To know you're not alone." I suddenly wanted to know how his eyeballs tasted. I wanted to lick his eyeballs, and I shuddered. "You don't know what I want!" I screamed and fled into the nearest dark alley. I had an affair with the flier off and on for twelve years. My husband never knew, or he knew enough to know I would never leave him permanently for those saltless cookies. The flier used to tell me I was wasting away at the bakery. He told me to embrace my true self. I told him people like us aren't made to be worshipped, to be martyrs, because that is for the soft-skinned, righteous, and desperate. He told me I liked to say things that didn't make any sense to sound deeper than I really am. After that I set the bed on fire. Then the bathroom. And his passport. He flew above me in circles of rage that only engorged the flames then called me a "cunt-swinging sack o' snatch." That left me unmoved, so he dared to use the V word. The fire went out of me like a sad song. I exited through the window and sat alone in the dark, trying to justify the connection between the martyrs (the soft skin, the silence, and the pain) and the life I knew (the lies and the butter). The metaphorical links failed in my head. I knew the location of every ingredient in the bakery better than I did the lies I told to keep me out of it. I always went back, maybe that was the silence. I still don't know. I texted him in the morning while at breakfast with my husband. He texted back one of those clever words for vagina, for villain, and my husband declared me in a good mood. We went on like that. We go on like that. Every day wet dough is put in my hands. The skin on my knuckles dries and thins year after year, and I feel the hot energy in the yeast as it wakes.

THERE ARE NO NINJAS
IN THE END

Big uncle told me it would be this way. Small uncle just sucks on caramel chews every moment he takes a breath. Mo didn't want an epidural because she didn't want the drugs to block the bonding process between her and the babies. She just keeps telling us she is dying and looking at us like we don't believe her and there is no hope, and it breaks my heart. All I can do is make promises and sip on a sweet drink for energy. She walks around because the midwives make her. Mo says she has to poop over and over. She has to have the babies. The twins, a boy and a girl, come out fast. The midwife passes each one quick, unceremoniously, onto a table. They lie there oily like two humongous fists that fell out of a mouth, unhappy and almost humiliated or robbed of something wonderful. Twins are freaky. They represent some epic balance, the dichotomy of good and evil, Mars and Venus dynamic, or the potential for a catastrophic error.

When I was nine, big uncle and small uncle took me in for good. They knew my mom before she loved other stuff more than me. Big uncle asked me who I would bring with me to the end of the world. I could bring only five people. Small uncle said he would bring four farmers and one soldier. I wanted to know how much of an end we were dealing with. Would there be Internet, working outlets, sludge in the faucets, gas stations, beef jerky, or energy drinks? How much would I have to give up? That would tell me who to bring. He said I had to give it all up. No more cream-filled cupcakes and Ninja Warrior reruns, and not even guns. When he took away the guns, I told him I didn't want to play anymore. He sucked the ass kick right out of the apocalypse. It made sense though, bullets are finite objects. Life can't be lived with something that no longer is in production. Eventually ammo runs out, parts don't get replaced. The apocalypse would be all combat, all day, rust skies over an ocean of corpses half decomposing from some mad, clever, bioterrorist attack. The borders between countries collapse as easily as the front doors to grocery stores that get looted and emptied, simple and messy like smashing a tomato on your mouth. It all seemed so uncomfortable. Then it happened. I saw the end of our lives as clear as opening the trunk of a car. There would be cake and tilapia when small uncle dies. I would have no feeling except in my ears. Big uncle will have fireworks.

Around month five and a half of the pregnancy Mo's cousin with the lisp and I started the emotional affair. After about thirteen days the emotional affair turned into a full-on, bare-assed affair. I liked it better when it was just cheating with our thoughts and feelings even though most people assume otherwise. During the feelings time Mo's cousin actually had a name. We emailed and texted. I had dreams about her that were eighty to ninety percent platonic. Then sex happened, and she turned into just this body with teeth that never touched properly.

The twins are born fine, no more and no less the babies a person with no imagination would expect. The lilt of their cries dissolves the muscle of me. My torso feels seized by the grip of a giant with its thumb pressed into my sternum. I can't name the feeling love or fear or anything. Thinking about Mo makes all of the usual sensations take over. Sex seems necessary right away. I mean right away. The obvious pending delay makes it that much more of an imperative.

When I met Mo she was one of those kinds of girls that scare other girls. She had big feet, drew eyeballs all over her notebooks, and walked with this fearless stride that never showed up in school pictures. I hated her for a long time because I knew I loved her, and she didn't love me yet. I told her about being raised by big uncle and small uncle. I told her how big uncle sits around conjuring up scenarios and asking crazy questions like he was gathering fragments for his own religion. I told her about the five people we get to bring to the apocalypse. She said she'd bring her cousins and her mom. That was it. Just them. I was mad again. It passed. Later, when we were older, we could think deeper about big uncle's nightmarish future worlds. There would be no more order, no guarantee of an end of any kind, so everyone would live especially hard in the moment, wishing. Hesitation would be a memory, impulsivity and remorselessness dominate.

After I told the uncles how we die, we never talked about it again. They believed me and the end of things didn't seem so mysterious or interesting. Big uncle decided to prepare for extraterrestrial invaders that would not destroy humanity but make reasonable changes involving lots of mating. Small uncle weighs more than big uncle, but he isn't long boned like him. They fostered me until we all loved each other for sure, I guess. The house in Phoenix is old, swamp cooler and all. Small uncle watches the home and garden channel all of the time, but the house still looks like hell. Mo liked it at my house better than hers despite everything. Her mom and dad were cops, minimalists. Her cousins were in gangs and treated her like a secret, something to keep hidden in doors where it is safe. The uncles believed in flavored teas, the healing power of houseplants, and walking shoes.

Mo always wanted to be a mother, especially when her mother became sick. I know she secretly didn't want to be pregnant and give birth, but she wanted her babies. Certain things freak her out. She can't look directly under a mushroom or watch shows about animals with two or more heads. The story about the little girl born with eight limbs just about made her faint. She broke out in a flop sweat when the doctor said twins. That's how the girl with eight limbs got all those extra parts, her sister. Mo was afraid every day for nine months about the nightmares she invented. She'd wake me up at night begging me to stop her from thinking. The thinking is what comes in so many gruesome layers. I was tempted to check, look into their lives and see how they end. Instead, I told her about one of big uncle's ideas. The environment. That's the monster we forgot. The monster of the future is a planet's revenge. The medusae, the earth stompers, and weather beasts are the next big threat. Mo asked, do they change the air? The environment couldn't be personified into a singular opponent, a thing with a face and heart and eyes. The concept was so much bigger than both of us and, most importantly, outside of Mo's body. That consoled her. When Mo found out the uncles were lovers and not brothers, she seemed relieved. No one shared blood in our house, and it fascinated her. We all got along. We weren't cursed with biological obligation. We don't fear the failings of family may one day take hold or be hereditary like bunions, cancer, narcissism, or desperation. Big uncle's obsession with the apocalypse wasn't about how the world stops, but how it starts again. Life is not the peak, two fists plunged high into the sky; it is the hard pull of preparation peppered with disappointments that vacuum the soul into dark pits so all that is left is the climb out and up toward redemption that may or may not exist, he says.

Mo accused me of blatant sabotage of our relationship, a juvenile destructive impulse programmed into me by GI Joe cartoons and caffeinated beverages. If I laughed in that moment, I was sure one look from her would make my tongue explode. Something that took years to create, our own miniuniverse was shaken from below for no reason. The cousin wasn't even the cute one. And Mo could not have a revenge affair equally painful because she was thick with babies, and I had no other family besides the uncles. She and I are not on good terms and may never be again. In the hospital room, small uncle just smiles with his mouth full of refined sugar and brown dye. Now the twins have to cope with the world but secretly miss that other life, violently taken away. An apology seemed due. I stare at them both, trying to determine which will be the good one and which one will be full of brine and attitude. Between them could be madness and genius, with me to help discern the difference. I want to know, divine the future because knowing helps planning, and planning staves off the throat knot of uncertainty. One of them sneezes. Then the other sneezes. I worry they might want to be just like me. They might be better or much worse. Even though the love felt at birth is dense and bright, that love might change, elongate, turn sallow enough for us to be glad when they fail to be more than we were at that age. I understand that knowing the end would be useful as knowing the origin of the seed that made my lemonade; it won't be any yellower, and it won't taste any better.

HOLD 'TIL WARM

The itch. The itch, the deep itch in his throat started. Clay always believed he could beat it. The virus, an opponent, had a handicap. All opponents have handicaps to be exploited. His parents taught him that. Clay had not seen his parents in four days, perfectly normal. Of course he could hear them in the early mornings and at night in their bedroom: laughter, the clinking of hard objects. Due to a bad student loan he still lived with his parents and worked at a young tech firm in the valley. He looked in the bathroom mirror. He had good teeth, good pecs, and an ebbing hairline appropriate for men in their late twenties. Despite the vitamins, the exercise, and the positive thinking, Clay was getting a cold. The charm that hung from the gold chain around his neck, a nude woman, Virgo, encircled with tiny sapphire stones, struck him as solution one. He put the charm in his mouth, under the tongue.

On the morning of that viral attack, Clay began to execute the usual tricks. He always believed he could make the cold go away before it became too late, before his throat felt like it were being scaled by a thousand demon fairies. First he swallowed unholy amounts of orange juice, vitamin C, and echinacea pills. The acidic juice burned, and he lost some hope. He rubbed Neosporin around his nostrils and gums like cocaine. Some false promise in his head kept him faithful to this routine. Still, his body warmed, and fatigue settled on his shoulders despite the simple medicine. He planned to ask Evie to breakfast, to impose the actions of a healthy man on his day, refuse to wear a sweater even though the chill ran deep along his neck or lie back down.

Meet in park? I bring coffee.

Can't. Will be late. Find Rachel, lunch maybe?

The disappointing texts made him throw his phone on the comforter in his bedroom. He headed to his parents' side of the house. The parents had their purposes, run then rocks. As geologists, rock brought them together, but not as much as their hardcore competitive inclinations. They ran marathons, approached every problem like a cramp on the sixth mile. Ease up, throw some water on your face, toss the cup at the most sinister-looking bystander, and push on. Pain can be managed later. Nothing matters but the finish. Their marriage hit a rough patch while Clay completed high school. Clay's grandfather died from a stroke, and his mother lost her faith in science. In his family, that was worse than sex with a student. She stopped using cell phones and digital coffeemakers. Without science Clay's parents had to find something else to share: mostly marijuana. It worked. They got good again, made dinners together, standing up in the kitchen. Leftovers stayed out for Clay when he came home from school, then college, then work. Clay ate most of the food, and they liked that. The refrigerator had dozens of alphabet magnets his parents used to deliver important messages: "The milk has turned." "Dentist, 4:30." "That guy you brought over last night smells like a boiling pot of anuses." "There will be pie!" Sometimes Clay left a response or set up a time to actually meet in person. This time he had to improvise. He found his parents that morning sitting at their desks in the office, perpendicular to each other, against the farthest corner of the room in true egalitarian fashion. Certificates and degrees lined the walls in no clear hierarchy. Photos of the two on various mountaintops in Colorado or Japan or on a Hawaiian volcano filled in the spaces between awards, declaring everything a challenge and triumph. Small limestone rocks halved to reveal the spectacular formations inside lay haphazardly about. A dozen slices of agate, amethyst, and Mexican coconut geodes that used to be Clay's crib mobile hung from the lamp shade in a corner. He let the charm fall from his mouth, the wet metal cold on his throat before entering. His mother wore pink and black track shorts with a V-neck tee. The sagging around her elbows made him want to hug her. Then he remembered why he came in. He turned to his father and saw his inordinately long legs coming out of a pair of cargo shorts covered in a mat of tight, black, curly hair and almost changed his mind. He turned to leave when his mother called him back.

"I'm sick."

"Aww, Claby, Claby, come here."

She pulled his face down to her without fully leaving her chair.

"This is exciting, Claby," she said. "We're all together here, talking, together like a family."

It seemed natural for his mother to treat the three of them like an experiment, like a Jane Goodall adventure whenever something banal as sickness occurred, they happened to sit down to watch a movie at the same time or gave each other rides to the airport. The goings-on of family life seemed remarkable as more than just life but as theoretical phenomena in action.

"We're here for you," his father said. "Whatever it is."

The sincerity in the posturing nearly drove Clay from the room. While his mother marveled at the group trial of family living, his father mocked it with clichés. Clay's mother sat upright after the brief pep talk from her husband and exercised a less carefree enthusiasm than she had before. Duty and the unyielding will to succeed gripped her. She pushed her rolling desk chair with one foot and slid over to her son, took him by the hand, and guided him to another chair, all without standing.

"Now," she said. "How are your glands?"

"When I was your age all kinds of shit started going wrong," his father began. "Woke up one day and keeled right over on the floor. Pain like a son of a bitch. Arches. My goddamn arches fell for no goddamn reason."

He took off his glasses as if committing to the moment for the first time.

"How long have you been sick, Claby? You could've left us a message."

Clay felt the truth forced on him. He hoped they would do most of the talking, work out the logistics of his illness, form a game plan, and then put it in motion. He hoped they would somehow know exactly why he was there, forgive him of his embarrassment, his averted gaze. Whatever they prescribed he would do, anything to make the pain of swallowing stop in his throat. He had not eaten.

"E.D. too," his father said. "That started about your age.

"Jesus!"

Clay's mother appeared to lose her clear analysis of the moment. Echoes of terror and ineptitude on how to proceed brought her eyebrows down. All of the flashes of poems, comforting phrases filed away from literature courses seemed not so useful. Love is truly an accident and can't be forced. To live below the trees, to fly, to be free and willing to accept what comes or doesn't is all there is because to force a bond will only bring the heat of loss and disappointment. She stopped in her chair, all movement, as if caught in a lie, a fraud uncovered. Like a dog walker masquerading as a plastic surgeon that had been getting away with it for decades but must now operate on a loved one, Clay's mother quit. Her son came to her mangled and needed her to make him better, and not even for the sake of her reputation as a capable surgeon could she risk much more than she had already. The stillness did not surprise Clay or his father. They knew the conversation had ended there, the experiment paused. His mother got up from her seat, touched Clay's arm, and left the room. She didn't leave with the urgency of some forgotten task. She left the room as if the room stopped being the room she needed to be in at all. His father put his glasses back on and returned to his rock specimens. Clay refused the sweater and left for work.

If only a hacking cough, only swollen glands, tear ducts run amuck, and mucus clogged sinuses were the worst of it. No. The isolation. The common cold equaled modern leprosy. Although never really said, a civilized person with a cold was required to keep a distance, self-sterilize, become a hermit for as long as necessary, and in essence become very, very small. Clay passed the park where he wanted to meet Evie, a place they'd known since childhood. In the parking lot at work, he noticed a peach pit on the walkway. It had not been there long, still had a few hairs of yellow and red peach meat on the spine of the pit. He picked it up, inspected a little; something always hidden inside made him clench it and look around before he made the decision. No one saw Clay at these times—not his parents, not Evie, no giant omnipresent idea of restoration and disappointment like God or the government seemed to be looking just then. With a last inspection he could see that one side of the seed had been smashed a little as if stepped on by a hard, flat shoe. He stood amazed that a peach pit could be flattened. The gnarled wood of it always seemed so invincible. People even call them stones. Once satisfied that he was alone, he put the seed in his mouth and held it. Soon Clay walked as usual with the thing rolling freely, knocking against his teeth, the almost tasteless metallic flavor seeping down his throat. A few people glanced at him with blind indifference; he could have been eating candy.

Clay sent Evie texts to meet for lunch that went unanswered. He shivered in the icy air-conditioning of the building. Three coworkers told him he looked like hell. Then he found her in the lunchroom. Evie walked over to Rachel, a young woman, interning for the fall. The three of them had drinks once at a private party. Clay almost interrupted when something stopped him. He experienced the transcendent hook in the soul shock that occurs when one human witnesses another in pain.

The room was empty except for Rachel, Evie, and almost Clay, who situated himself under the door frame. Rachel sat at the plain, white table with connecting benches, swollen-faced and watery-eyed. Clay knew of Rachel only through Evie, but he knew right away she had no consciousness of herself. Some people are more aware of the dragonflies colliding with window panes twenty feet away than they are of their own fingertips and earlobes. Rachel had that absent body quality. Her mind stayed there in the moment, but the body might as well have been wrapped in cellophane, dipped in honey, and sent rolling over a field of snack crackers. She carried her tablet around like an afterthought and constantly searched the walls and ceiling for who knows what. Evie had no confidence in her approach of Rachel and carried a carton of eggs, which seemed odd enough to make Clay hang back. The walk of uncertainty and regret led Evie to the same table as Rachel but the farthest point away. They could have been in different cities with their thoughts clearly on one another. Clay saw Rachel harden; her face dried and gained focus. The two didn't look at each other and did not notice Clay. Evie settled into her customary hunched-over position, common among the tech women, then slid the carton of eggs down to Rachel with a little too much force. The carton glided cleanly off the edge and Rachel made no effort to stop it. No disastrous clatter of ruptured shells and broken yolks ensued. Hard-boiled.

"Smooth," Rachel said.

Evie looked relieved to have been spoken to, acknowledged at all. Rachel picked up the carton and inspected the contents. Just then Clay realized he was watching an apology, an apology via gift of protein. With one hand Rachel de-shelled one of the boiled eggs and moved the carton a little. "No salt," she said.

"Fuck salt."

They both smiled, and Evie took that as an invitation to join the meal. They ate together. For the first three eggs each they didn't glance up, but by the fourth egg they increased speed and consumption, reaching for the next egg faster and more methodically while they kept close eye contact. A race had started. The two avoided the crumbling clay yolks and concentrated on the dense whites, a habit of women to avoid the fattiest parts, Clay considered. They chewed out of synchronicity but matched breaths. Overwhelmed at the sight of the blunt ends of the eggs bitten and restored, bitten and restored, Clay felt a rush of blood inside and needed something soon to hold in his mouth. A quick scan of the floor around him turned up nothing thanks to an extremely competent janitorial staff. He had eleven cents in his pocket and a ten-dollar bill. The thought of the coins repulsed him because he craved a different texture, something yielding and pliable. Clay folded the bill as tightly as he could with as little motion as possible so he wouldn't be spotted. At last the square of paper sat between his molars, and he could feel the pointy edge with the side of his tongue begin to dull. Before the last egg Evie put both feet on top of Rachel's under the table, perhaps to stop her from winning, perhaps to hold her in place, or perhaps to remind her that they were both real and present and in that room together. After the final swallow between them Evie shouted, "Seven!"

"You always win," Rachel said, having difficulty with her last bite.

"I mess up sometimes."

They went quiet. Clay turned away and into the hall as the two laughed about a Tabasco sauce incident. The soft dollar felt like a tiny quilt from the many indentations left by his teeth. In the hall Clay met another friend, Malachi. It was Malachi's party that introduced Evie to Rachel at all. Some people have issues with boundaries, knowing when not to get too close, knowing how close is too close, knowing that closeness is a privilege and not a right. Malachi knew no boundaries and had no friends other than Clay because of that. He had careless bathing habits, but threw good parties.

"Brought you a sub," Malachi said and gifted Clay a foot-long sandwich across his stomach. "You look shitty, man. Are you dying?"

One week ago Malachi gave a party at his home, his aunt's house, but she flew to Florida to plan a mission to the Ivory Coast with her church. At the party Malachi seemed the skilled alchemist while bartending, each cocktail promised transformation, life eternal. He served as the Bacchus of the firm, seductive, goat-legged leader of the blissful and the eager to be lost. At the party he scanned his aunt's living room and found much to be proud of among his inebriated coworkers: no fighting, no screaming, no evidence of vomit or theft (yet), just music and the communal dream that everything is beautiful therefore they should dance. In the small, ranch-style house built in the fifties, every crack and scrape on the walls and corners of doors revealed layers of paint and forgotten home fashion. The old furniture had weary springs, split seams, and all the drowsy comfort that brought along. Evie and Rachel sat together on a sofa. Clay wanted to be nice to Rachel because Evie liked her. He brought drinks, asked about family, complimented her socks; she confessed they were also toe socks and wiggled her feet outside of the shoe. He said she just blew his mind, and in that moment that was true. Evie kissed Rachel first or not. Rachel kissed Evie back or first. In either memory, Clay left the party alone.

In elementary school Evie played with Clay at the park near his house when his parents needed him out. They used to fight and then said they need to kiss to feel better. Evie and Clay patrolled the park more than played in it, surveying the new kids as they tumbled and screamed. Clay got the flu one day from chewing gum he found stuck on the swing chain. When he saw things like the gum, a panic took over, a dizzying confusion. The gum was too tough to manipulate with his tongue and roof of his mouth, but soon it warmed and slid around like a jewel. Evie yelled at him then called him a garbage eater, so he pushed her down. She ran home yelling garbage eater over her shoulder. Clay did not let her see him that way again.

After work, the cold gripped Clay hard. He walked into his home hoping for an invasion, some ski-masked lunatic with a nervous finger would shoot him in the face. He hurt all over. The sick sweat came in merciless waves. He closed the front door behind him, no intruders present. Clay found a message on the refrigerator: COLD MEDS BY SINK.

Clay called Evie to say I'm sick. She said she had laundry to finish. Evie put up barriers between them that looked like the stuff of life. Plus Evie and Clay were friends, meaning they grew up together and had become accustomed to being in each other's presence, so she came over, eventually. Clay finished two bowls of soup, took a shower, and watched half of a movie about extraterrestrial larvae before falling asleep. He thought he felt a kick. Evie stood over him, holding a can of lemon-fresh Lysol near his face.

"Don't talk or I'll gas you."

After spraying down the entire room, she sat in the chair beside the sofa, and they watched a half-hour show that described how factories produce plastic water bottles, pencils, and fire-retardant insulation. After the show, Clay threw off the blanket and knelt down at Evie's feet. He held her knees under each heavy palm. She looked at him incredulously as if he were suddenly something else, a hydrant or a Labrador. Clay made his intentions clearer, pressing his hands down on the tops of Evie's feet, sliding them up, then unbuttoning her jeans. She allowed it, that much, said nothing in words. Clay did not believe in doom, in impermanence, or failure by chance. Everything once lost waited to be revived. Even death mirrored a lie to be retracted.

To him, the burn of disappointment echoed a myth. He needed to live below the trees. The two had been partitioned by air and clothes and fear and protocol and habit. Clay wanted more, sank his head onto the fabric of Evie's lap. She touched him, the first time all day. The touch continued, and then it ended. She slid from under his head, rebuttoned, turned the volume down on the television, picked up the fallen blanket. She took his empty soup bowl to the kitchen and returned with water and a few of the pills his parents set out.

"Take these in an hour. You'll sleep better."

RAVISHED

He absolutely killed me: ravished. Their mother loved idioms, coaxed life back into the dead slang of generations past; cool beans, groovy daddy-o, and douche bag all had a place at the table, the breakfast table where she often discussed termite tracks along with her nightly rendezvous. "Killed me" always meant something wonderful, but ravish was the sisters' favorite. Ravished. "Ravished," they whispered into their cereal bowls. The milk moved under breath. Though still alive then, their mother was scrubbed bare like an antique candle-stick holder restored in the morning and tarnished by midnight, a candle holder, wearing a pink, terry cloth robe with knots of gray lint from her daughters' hoodies.

Some mothers are too big for cemeteries, their presence cascades out and up like history, like algae. The sisters put her in the grave and never looked back, not because their mother didn't deserve it but they could find her elsewhere. Mother, sister, daughter, miser, hooker, soccer coach, thief, apartment dweller, dog hater, agoraphobe, lady cuckold, savior, and friend would've cost too much by the letter on a tombstone. They celebrated her birthday no matter what, rock climbing in the Sierra Nevada, moose hunting in Alaska, and online double-dating, which was not too unlike shooting the moose, which they didn't. It was the buying of gear, the preparation, the ritual, and the distance that mattered most. But they ran out of ritual and youth and money and eventually turned to tequila in random parking lots. This year, a favorite, the 24-hour Laundromat; the hypnotic hum of the spinning machines calmed them.

I wanted it badly, one told the other—what—to be ravished. The other spit out her booze in a soft dribble. Me, too, even though it seemed like a horrible thing—it is a horrible thing—and not—it's when a bunch of kittens claw at the air all around your body—you thought that?—Of course—no, it's when you fall down together in leaves and roll around and splash until it feels like drowning—it's when a boy does karate kicks around your head but always misses— it's football—it's when you run together on a beach riding horses— white horses—Clydesdales—no, it's when you can't see because he's got his hands over your eyes, and there is a surprise waiting—it's when you have to go to the doctor and the doctor takes blood and the blood goes in the tube and he looks you right in the face and smiles and you want to throw up—it's when you throw up on your doctor—on your boyfriend—who is a doctor—it's when you agree to be somewhere at the same time, but he doesn't show up so you drink brandy in a cocktail dress on the porch till mosquitoes make you go back inside. They stopped. They considered how far they had not gone still, the lives they were supposed to be living on behalf of the dead. They considered the laundry and the moose, unkilled, still frolicking, roaming, and living that good moose life.

NOT LIKE YOU, NOT AT ALL

Not to be rude, but I was married to a man like you in my twenties. He was beautiful, and we were jealous, jealous of everyone, kissing fish that suck and drown. We built a pretty cage for ourselves with bougainvillea-entwined lattice and had sex a lot to keep from talking. Sometimes he spoke of joining the army like his father, but he was lazy as fog and became too old. For nine years we had eye-jittering sex four times a day. Then I married Eddie. He could make orange marmalade seem outright hilarious. Together we'd laugh anywhere like children during church. Strangers stared and smiled, but we couldn't stop. The cancer licked his skin bacon raw. When the ICU was full, and his father folded in a chair, nephews at the foot of the bed, odd, fuzzy, ginger-headed cousins from some nameless planet coughing in the doorway, and he lay pressed in the lasagna layers of hospital blankets, he'd put my hand on his crotch. The laughter came wrung out against my will like sugar, like sweat, like a whole child, like oil from a grape seed, an unlikely miracle. I miss him. You don't look anything alike.

ANNIE OAKLEY GUN
TRAINING FOR WOMEN

Grandma Goode, GG I call her, collects people, mostly old people from the classes she teaches at the range, Annie Oakley gun training for women. The class was held at the Black Canyon range, an open-air facility carved into the side of Dreamy Draw Mountain, formerly known as Squaw Peak—archery clinic held once a month, trap and skeet for youth on first and third Fridays, and, of course, the Cactus Pear shotgun program for ages nine and up. The range was vast and dusty, and pops of gun powder scattered through the air. Sunsets dripped and ran over the mountains like crimson wax. My eyes always stung after an hour in the stalls, but how could I not love it? All of GG's classes had the same running theme that always brought wounded women together in the name of self-defense: fear. She taught me how to shoot at eleven and said the same thing then that she always says after the first round of instruction when everyone goes out and takes a place on the range. Think about the thing you would destroy, the thing you fear the most, the thing that if you had a magic eraser you would wipe away forever; see it clear on the target, remember to breathe, then squeeze. Before firing at the paper plate taped on the block, I always saw mushrooms, not the cooked and sliced kind, the dank and growing kind.

It was Saturday night, and GG threw one of her shindigs for the latest group to celebrate their time together. This was not the house I grew up in. Here the walls were satin, white, stretching high up out of view, punctuated with iron suns and moons and the stenciled Kokopelli that came with the house GG meant to paint over because it annoyed her, the ancient trickster, the symbol of fertility and excess, debauchery and cunning, the southwestern cliché, the one thing she never got around to removing. Beveled, chocolate Saltillo tile on the floor made every step feel uneasy yet peaceful. Four guests anchored themselves on the cream leather sectional, leaning to the air just outside the patio doors, and shifting aside the fraying afghan I used to sleep on as a child. Three others hovered over the antique side table. A painting hung over the travertine fireplace. It was given to GG years ago by a Hopi artist who shot her husband in the stomach. I think the couple is still together. There were no cowboys and Indians in the image, just blustering arcs of yellows and reds. The woman said it was the story of her people, and I wanted to believe her, but it just looked like she did, shapes and colors in violent patterns. This was a house for show.

GG let me "tend the bar," as she says. A young woman should know her way around a cocktail, always emphasizing the cock. Our private joke, emphasis on the private, that she thought damned funny. I did, too. So at seventeen I could make an old-fashioned, a proper martini, and understood the importance of stocking up on bitters. Once I tried to make vermouth out of wine bottle dregs simmered with herbs and brandy, but it tasted like rancid spaghetti, ass, and bad luck. GG's home would've been better suited to a bed and breakfast brochure in Oaxaca, Mexico, instead of a cul-de-sac in a North Phoenix subdivision. The candle sconces put a gold film over the guests that made every eye deep and pulsing. I rubbed the martini glasses with a cloth because it made me look bartenderish, which I liked. A part should be played well. I even wore a bow tie and white shirt and stood behind the counter on a step stool. GG's actual bar was separate from the kitchen, complete with a mirror backsplash above the sink and shelves of pretty liquors most guests admired from a distance while sipping midlevel vodka. For some reason this bunch had a high percentage of shellfish allergies, so GG, of course, ordered tray upon tray of crab cakes and shrimp skewers. Paying attention was never her thing. She could irk people because of that fervent disregard for instructions, always had the expression of somebody listening intently and aimed to please, but the end result was a wondrous misunderstanding.

Then I saw the one, the one guest not over a hundred years old and not full of stories about wars and gas prices that are really somehow just about sex and how they are proud they can still do it. She had on this miniskirt with leather trim and a no-sleeve white blouse with a modest neckline and these stockings almost red but not really. It was like two halves of two really great outfits put together in a way that was all wrong and just right, but she had no idea one way or the other. This girl had to be older, roughed-up enough by life to take shooting classes with grown-ups and order a drink. I knew the drink she'd ask for, amaretto sour, something tart and sweet and sure to bring on a healthy buzz if made the good way. I could make it that way. GG let me taste test when she taught me her secrets. I taste tested all evening during these parties between sips of water. The bourbon and tequila flowed without beginning or end until I saw her, that one girl, moving among the aged collection like in a museum. The alcohol broke apart in my blood and traveled out of my stomach, awakening the cells. I could feel my knees and my collarbone, brain reveling in the dimmed reality. She cleansed me in that softened light and brought the sound to tolerable levels. Each of GG's collection posed like ancient treasures encased in velvet rope or hung on white walls, except these sculptures were alive and spoke of many things. The pair at the side table passed around ideas on war. The sofa echoed of sex and divorce. Then there was GG and Douglas, the terrorist she calls him, near the patio door. "Heard on the news that a man grew a pea sprout in his lung," GG said, "and I threw up." "He had a slight cough," Douglas replied.

GG had explosive power on her hip but the vocal cords of a paper crane. She didn't have on the .357 magnum revolver tonight, but she carried it everywhere, that six-inch, chrome barrel with a wooden grip too big for my hand but not for hers; she loved the size, the thunder of firing, the imposing awe of it holstered at her side like a jeweled scarab, as if she were Scheherazade in *The Thousand and One Nights*, but in this version the heroine doesn't have to tell stories to save her life; her future is already secured. There were stoppers and slowers. A .22 is for slowing, the rounds will lodge in tissue or bone or sometimes travel and ricochet through the body like a pinball. A .357, however, is for stopping, no apologies, no recourse, finite as the grave. Douglas co-instructed the training courses with GG, and if she collected people, Douglas collected their stories. *What are you aiming at?* he asked them. They told, each tale more terrible than the next, the runaways, the slaves, the home invasions, the battered wives that ran out of excuses. There was the cousin of an artist in India who had been chopped up and stored in cardboard boxes. I'd heard too many and stopped hearing the party chatter at all except for GG. I wanted to show this girl to her, let her see what I saw, thank her for being so thoughtful and inviting someone interesting for once. It kind of fell apart in my head when I realized what GG might say. She would make it all about fear and how I should face it, and just hearing that I would run. She would make the girl this whole, vast, threatening prospect. It wouldn't look like love at all anymore. Other people outside of the classes had more manageable fears to begin with, so facing those seemed practical. Anyone could be afraid of heights then go bungee jumping and say, *Well, that was no big deal.* The arachnophobia-stricken can just pick up a tarantula one day, feel the near weightless fragility of it and get on with their lives. I did not like the idea of facing any of it, preferred a side glance. I was too old. People should be exposed to things like mushrooms at an earlier age, that way they'd be desensitized. Not too long ago, hangings were family events. You don't want to wait until children are nearly adults before you introduce death and cruelty. They might not know how to handle it, might develop inappropriate fascinations. I had to be nearly eight years old before I saw death up close.

GG and I were in the backyard, a small space, closed in by the garage and a pink brick fence. We had lazy birds of paradise that couldn't hold their blossom heads upright. A sunflower grew from a seed I pushed in the ground with my thumb; it made a stalk thick as my wrist with almost no help from me other than that first touch. Corn, wilting strawberries, a pomegranate tree barely taller than me all held up the corners of the yard. In the middle we had grass that GG was about to teach me how to mow. That morning after a heavy rain the sharp grass made spongy noises underfoot like stepping on a wet broom. GG screamed, *Ahhh, look at these.* In my mind I was suddenly there, right next to her, without running or anything. I saw the mushrooms in a cluster. I screamed, too. I went to hide my face in GG's back, but she kept turning to see me so we twirled in circles, a backyard dervish of terror and amusement like a married couple deranged by time and circumstance. GG held my head and spoke into my hair. She had the floral smell of Jean Naté and a little mud. She said they're always there in the dirt. You don't have to plant them. The idea that these complicated monstrosities could grow from nothing in a matter of hours gave me no peace. Some wicked sprite had to be in charge, something fourteen feet tall made of corn husks and ice water coughed on our grass and left behind a maddening development. Inside the house my mother was sleeping off the handful of Vicodin she'd had for breakfast; she slept her deepest sleep ever.

During the party a man's voice began to sing beautifully then badly, and there was laughter. Messy plates shifted in the tiny sink behind me. The walls softly expanded and contracted; it was like being eaten alive. I thought to ask the girl to dance, but her eyebrows stopped me. Her eyebrows. They were wide as the bristles on my toothbrush. Enormous. Adorable even though older women aren't supposed to be adorable, I don't think. But they were that. I glanced at my own carefully constructed outfit and was reminded that I was a servant that night. My mind sought out safer refreshments rather than booze. GG's coffeepot always murmured like an obese seductress. I suddenly wanted to write poetry longhand with beautiful penmanship and communicate clearly, and with sensitivity, but I could think only sugar packets. Pink packets. Blue packets. Raw sugar. White. Jars of powdered creamer and the better kind in liquid form. Cinnamon. I liked that people used it even though the thought of having it in my own was repulsive. We always had tea of many colors—green, black, chai, Earl Grey, oolong even. Oh, oolong. It all made my blood swell. The seconds ticked on, and I was losing the battle of credibility. Soon my skeleton would abandon the whole spectacle altogether and leap out through a single pore on my forehead. I had no poetry in me. My handwriting looked like dirty ants wrestling.

A glob of peach pie hit the tile like a slap on the ass. A tiny huddle of guests whistled. The thing about old people is that they see how fantastic a disappointment the world is turning out, and deep down inside they know it's all their fault. This doesn't make for a particularly regretful segment of the population. Somehow they become mischievous and crafty. I could imagine every one of them climbing trees and casting spells in moldy, scented forests, Douglas certainly, an incantation for every strip of pain recorded in his memory bank of tragic tales. GG seemed especially likely to have a cauldron of crow feathers and squirrel toes simmering somewhere always. Whatever brew GG made would have healed something for sure.

Like a spirit, the girl appeared in front of me inquiring about something, something I wanted to give her but could not shrink my pupils or dull the pounding in my ears long enough to understand.

"Can you?" she asked.

"I'm sorry."

"Can you make a Cadillac margarita ha?"

The doubt she expressed cut me in half. I let my muscle memory take over, but the Grand Marnier went missing. I found it. I made her order. Strong, but not obvious. She declared it good and motioned for me to follow her to the sofa. She bent her shoulders low in a gesture of supplication, and I yielded. When I stepped from the stool, she was taller all of a sudden then laughed again. The halves of me followed.

"You look too young to be in the class. I'm Holly, Douglas's granddaughter."

Again, the apparition of Holly moved from a relatively safe distance on the sofa to right against me. I spent unnecessary seconds trying to remember how Holly got so close so fast. Some people become garrulous and flirty when lightly intoxicated; Holly was one of those people. She sat down as if she had a dozen epic novels to recite, including the acknowledgments and appendices, because each word was a huge scandal and needed to be shared immediately. Some other kinds of people become pensive and docile when intoxicated. I was that kind of person.

"My granddad just loves Mrs. Goode. He says she hasn't got a clue. NOT A CLUE! Ha. He just thinks her class is the best thing ever. Don't believe anything different. I swear that man is a son of a bitch. SON OF A BITCH! I really love that tie. Where did you get it? And don't tell me you don't remember. I say that all the time. ALL THE TIME!"

Douglas spotted Holly and me on the sofa. She pressed the knot of my tie lower then lifted it back up, liking it better that way. I began plotting a method to discourage him from joining us. His presence seemed a disastrous prospect. Then I thought about the old man and the pea sprout and felt dizzy. The old man didn't bother me much, not even his heavily oxygenated lung really. It was the possibility the event illuminated in my mind. I drew lines around things, charcoal borders that separate what needs separation. Plant life, especially plant life, and certain nondigestive human organs needn't ever meet, but they had, and the union was fruitful. The doctors removed the sprout, but what if they hadn't? What if other people inhale peas and never notice? Could that happen to GG someday? What if her sprout continued to do what nature wanted, and all she complained about was a slight cough. Her lungs would become webbed and braided with vines; heart punctured eventually but with such deft precision and slow movement that the meat of her just fuses to the roots. Even after death and her body is mourned, returned to the ground, the roots grow deeper, breaking her embalmed skin, breaking the breast buttons of her favorite white suit, breaking the leather of her holster and that .357 she asked to buried with, breaking the wood of the casket, breaking the packed surface to emerge with fleshy edible blossoms that when blown by the wind gently cough.

I tried to stop terrifying myself for a minute and will my body sober, but Douglas pressed on. I watched the space around his body like trying to make out the blurry parts of a photograph. Behind him a woman helped herself to tequila at the bar, refilling her glass before smashing two limes onto the rim, graceless. I needed to be there to restore order. Douglas continued to approach, and I stood straight up ready to flee back to my post. Holly took my hand with an expression of disapproval, and I suddenly remembered how to speak. She was brand-new and beautiful and uncoordinated in her speech and clothing and deserved all my adoration for those reasons.

"Sorry," I said and sat back down because I wanted to, and the liquor now in my marrow said it was okay.

GG intercepted Douglas before he could reach the sofa. She winked at me, and I felt the blood crashing in my face.

"There's nowhere to go ha," Holly said.

"Holly."

"I'm right here. You're so funny. I like that."

Holly tilted her knees against mine as she bent down to pull a corner of the afghan around her ankles, the night turning chill only because she never took more than the first sip from her drink. She slid a thumb along the condensation.

"Did you like the class?" I asked her.

"NO. Don't get me wrong. Grandad took me to learn from Mrs. Goode, REALLY does love her, I think. I put it off for years though. I just don't believe in GUNS. I KNOW, weird company I keep. Does that make you hate me?"

Holly almost took my hand then made a fist against her own thigh. I told her I did not hate her, but said the night wasn't over.

"You're being nice," she replied, squeezing my hand for a second without thinking. "I know, how can YOU not like them? I was a baby, so I don't care, and he tells everybody all the time but not like he does all the others' stories. If you're cornered, and he's had enough whiskey, then you get the details. We're not supposed to TALK about death. It's a thing. You talk about it, and that's an invitation."

"I don't think he believes that."

"You're right or . . . well, she was killed at a gas station in Detroit. Actually, not killed, hit, stray bullet. Bastards probably didn't even know she was there, my mother. I was in the car, a baby, I don't remember it. She drove while bleeding to death and stopped in front of a hospital." Holly pulled and straightened her blouse casually, speaking as she might about the weather. "She got that far, didn't make it out, was there for hours before someone heard me crying. No point in reporting any of it, not how it works, I guess. We moved to Arizona after."

At the moment I wished desperately to remember all of what I'd been told, knew it was important, but couldn't determine why exactly. Holly had handed me a horror story, but all I could feel was happy. Something had been explained. Something I didn't know I should know, but in the moment I was only aware of Holly's shifting weight on the sofa, the lint she pulled from my pants, and hair she pushed from her face. The wine glass floated in and out of my hand. Holly put down her own glass and began sipping carelessly out of mine. The night had clipped on, and it was time for music. GG turned on the stereo, classical Indian songs full of moaning strings and hypnotic chants. Not everyone immediately understood the choice, and no one danced. It didn't seem a party for that intention at all. Standing alone seemed too much for some of the guests. With a dutiful exhale, Holly rose and held up a finger to me as if to say, *Don't go anywhere; I'll be right back.* Her eyebrows bent like handlebars headed off on a happy, urgent mission. I was alone for what seemed like half a second, but enough to feel pitiful, abandoned, and too drunk to fake self-confidence. I looked for GG, listened for her, but there was nothing and no one to protect me from the room, only Douglas now moving freely towards me across the tile, almost afloat like something sliding on a tongue. Then he sat down.

"So, young lady, what do you aim at?"

I felt I could talk for hours like I'd been resting up for it. I told him all about mushrooms, their spores, yes, the spores, but the environment makes the difference. I knew more than I ever wanted to about a variety of fungi. Truthfully the full canon of mushrooms is quite inventive and horrific. *Agaricus bisporus* is the white button mushroom most people think of with the plain straight stem and brown gills on the underside of the cap. Oh, but there are others. *Amanita muscaria* is the mushroom of lore and legend with a slick, bright red cap, pretty as an apple mottled with white patches, which elves abuse as furniture. A *leucocoprinus birnbaumii* or yellow pot mushroom once grew to the size of a small cabbage in my childhood home. It birthed beside a house plant when I was almost fourteen. GG adored that fat fungus and kept it hidden, but when I saw it I cried and refused to come back in the house. Maybe she thought it was a sign, a way to take care of something lost to her. Eventually GG gave in, broke the mushroom into halves and quarters with a garden spade. It was young, just pale, dense meat like grapefruit rind. She carried it outside in a plastic grocery bag, and I could breathe again.

Mushrooms eat. They consume organic matter unlike a plant. There is no photosynthesis, no poetic transformation of blank light into energy and air. Many are edible: chanterelles with their golden potato chip caps, shiitake, oyster, enoki, crimini, and portobello. Some have gorgeous names: earthstars, truffles, hen of the woods, bird's nests, puffball, stinkhorn, jellies, and toadstools. Some can even possess the minds of insects; turn them into scorned deranged lepers of their colonies where they scurry to high ground until the monster in their brains literally bursts out. Others less bold and more deadly are for enemies. *Amanita phalloides* is the death cap. It looks deceptively like any plain, fruit-bodied mushroom, white with a touch of green. Half a cap is enough to kill a man. They are rumored to be delicious.

The day GG and I found the mushrooms outside, after finishing the yard work, I went inside alone. Everything seemed normal except the carpet, boggy and wet. My mother left the kitchen faucet running after a junkie's half-attempt at doing dishes. I turned it off and treaded through the squishy hall into her bedroom. In the dark only sharp pins of sunlight entered. The rest is only a dream for those who don't believe in aliens and angels. I opened the door to the bedroom because the seams around the frame were pressed with light. Inside, regardless of what is true, what is dream, and what is memory, I saw the tiny room barely big enough for the bed in the center and the wood dresser by the door, filled with yellow pots. The mushrooms lined the corners of the wall and blanketed the floor. From the middle of the floral comforter on the bed they bubbled forth. I could almost hear them living, the oldest cracking open and releasing black spores, the youngest still soaking up water and swelling happily. Her body was present, but my mother was not there anymore; she was everywhere. I collapsed backward into the hall. The discovery left me pressurized, the inner tube of my body stretched to capacity. This was my first trip alone into the world, something I thought improbable but not impossible like touching the moon until you find a piece in an exhibit. There is the moon (a small chunk) and not only has it been touched, it's been touched by everyone, licked by children, dismissed by grown men, fondled, sneezed upon. It has been touched so frequently and without reverence that it seemed sick. The next improbable but not impossible task would be to put the moon back where it might heal.

At the dinner party many of the guests were leaving or had left. I rolled the flute between my thumb and forefinger. Two shades of lipstick on the rim. Douglas smiled like a Greek emperor who had lost his empire but escaped with his life. In the light he had no eyes and very well could have been the marble bust of a handsome nobleman.

"Don't believe anything that drunk lesbian tells you," he said.

"You mean your granddaughter?" I replied.

"That's right."

"Then you aren't a son of a bitch?"

Holly came back at a pace slower than when she left, one hand flat against her skirt, the other holding something behind her back, and eyes full of relief. I expected her to return fully assembled, tightened up, and adjusted, but instead she had unbuttoned her blouse, taken off her shoes to carry them on a single finger, the wick of her exposed at head and toe. When she saw me watching, she drew a breath, and I knew the room had devoured me, but here was the rebirth, a mess of good intentions.

"Ask her to dance," he told Holly.

"Granddad!"

"Yes, ask me."

I could see GG now. She'd been there all along, bent over her laptop that linked to the stereo. She'd been trying to change the music for twenty-five minutes. I left her to it. Douglas, Holly, and I went out to the veranda, and in the dry cold twirled together, our feet tracing small phrases into the dust.

SCARS

The pitcher just struck out Esperanza, so right then redemption was up to me. I have the biggest legs of all the Lady Mantises. Daddy used to always say people here like it when you can do something special but not too special. Our town isn't really small. We don't have rolling hay fields or anything like that. It's not big, either, though. Teenagers like me and T don't have much going on; of course, there is more to do than go shopping and get pregnant. There's softball.

I tried to give Esperanza a look, something that said "don't worry about it. You did your best. The pitcher has an arm like a moose's throat. You're still incredible and everybody knows it." I tried to make the face Daddy used to make when I struck out, but Esperanza didn't look back. My sister, T, yelled and threw random things around the dugout. "How did you miss that pitch?!" T screamed. "The ball is the size of a monkey's skull. She threw it so slow it might as well have had a monkey attached to it!" Esperanza curled up like a five-foot-ten potato bug. Coach Watson always lets T get away with chewing out the rest of us. Coach had thick furry arms and smelled good enough to follow anywhere. Esperanza told me once that it's bad luck to have a team name that ends with an S. I want to be slim like T. We're only ten months apart, but she's the golden tree, and I'm the brown shrub.

—

Before his accident, Daddy used to bring me and T to our games. Now Mama does it since she doesn't trust us with the car—says our minds wander. At Daddy's funeral she told Pastor Short she felt surrounded by dark spirits. Pastor Short knew how to lay hands on his congregation to push the dark spirits away. Pastor Short had a degree in dark spirits. Pastor Short was the dark spirit whisperer.

It was an accident, how Daddy died: sleep apnea. That's when you just about choke to death every night but wake up just in time to stay alive. That doesn't happen always—the waking up, I mean. Everything T and I knew got split into halves, before the accident and after. Before, Daddy helped us train. I was up to three hundred pounds on the leg press. Now I can barely do 180. Before, T had to run three miles a day just to prove to Coach she deserved to be a Lady Mantis. Now she's out of breath running from first to third and gives the rest of us shit for missing impossible pitches. After Daddy's funeral T asked me how many people had on white hats. I told her three. She thought about it. "How many people didn't have on a tie?" Forty. "How many guys, dumb ass?" T clarified. Just our twin cousins Ronald and Donald. She said I was right. We learned something new then. Pain helped us remember. Soon we taped needles to pen caps so we could prick our fingers in class. Sometimes I let the needle scrape just under my thumbnail or harder between my knuckles. If it bled too much I had to wait. Our grades improved.

———

T made up this game for just the two of us. We each get points for injuries. The worst are called diamonds and get us one thousand points easy. Small hurts are peanuts and get only twenty-five or less. Anything more than that we have to debate.

After Esperanza's strikeout, I was up. The other team chanted "Lady Bug Slugs." Girl with the moose-head arm let a fast one go. No matter what happened I was going to connect. I swung for all of us: me, T, Daddy and Esperanza. I hit the ball. I hit the ball with my left elbow. Before impact I knew I was getting a diamond. The bone disintegrated like a dandelion in a breeze. Except instead of petals of fluff I got vomit-inducing pain that spread from shoulder to heel. I busted only my elbow but everything hurt. It was like my body forgot which part was broken and said, "To hell with it. She's all messed up." T was right. The pain helped our memories. T and I might not be so special. Maybe we're the opposite of lucky. Most people spend their whole lives trying to avoid every uncomfortable feeling. For us, discomfort was the only thing that put a face on the clock. Time is just a wobbly, blank surface full of smoke. Pain made the wind blow and the ground still.

—

T claimed some of her points just because. One night we heard a couple of cabinets slam in the kitchen. She went to investigate. T came back with a box of raisins, and said she caught Mama with her hand on Pastor Short's crotch. Said it looked like she was trying to open a drawer with an awkward handle. T claimed fifty for that. I said okay. After T had sex her first time with the Coach she said she earned twenty. I said okay. T made fun of me for my crush on Esperanza in a way that said I feel sorry for you, but you're safe here. Esperanza had eyes like a bush baby and really sharp incisors. When I saw her hug Gerald Preston after Mantis practice I wanted to claim a million. I never said anything.

—

In midcollapse from the ball collision, I got that clarity people talk about when they talk about death. I saw the twenty-seven pairs of green eyes, ninety brown ones, twelve blue and fourteen gray in the stands. Two men screamed, "You're a goddamn liar" simultaneously. Pastor Short applied a layer of lip balm with his pinky. T hated him for her own reasons. They weren't mine. Coach Watson took off his cap. I knew that one day when I got older and somehow felt bigger, and there were no more secrets between us, I would remember him almost never.

My mother stood in the shade, so I couldn't make out her head. Whatever unnamed muscle of parental affection inside her was weaker than my daddy's. I wanted better but settled on forgiveness.

A mosquito plunged its blood tube into Esperanza's wrist as she brought her hand to her mouth in eye-watering shock. Right then I knew she loved me, too. T inhaled a popcorn kernel and proceeded to choke on it. I was happy. Esperanza asked the EMT if I would be okay. He said, "Fuck yeah, but she caught a good one." With those super big, round, animal eyes Esperanza looked at me for a number of searing gorgeous seconds and mouthed the words "good luck" before the ambulance doors closed. Commercials for doughnuts and erectile dysfunction played on the car radios that passed. Incomprehensible conversations of babies echoed in the hospital. The clock in the stadium read 5:16 p.m. when the ball hit. The nurse gave me Percocet at 5:44 p.m. Things got fuzzy after that. That barbed wire whisk that made scrambled eggs out of my arm showed me the thin layer between true consciousness and sleep. Turns out a needle, a casket, or a monkey skull all had the power to make real and firm every dim, impermanent thing, for a little while.

RUN AWAY SCREAMING

Texas. 1974. Ms. Anne pissed herself all over the passenger side of Duncan's pickup truck one morning. This was quite normal except for one other thing. Ms. Anne belonged to the foreman on-site, but she was a friend to Duncan and proud as any twenty-four-year-old ginger cat could be. She always had that I-messed-up-but-I-just-can't-help-myself look in her dull, slanted eyes. Duncan never complained or cursed or mumbled as he wiped up the piss (sometimes shit) that Ms. Anne let dribble from her rear, off the leather and onto the floor. He'd even get a little warm water and wash Ms. Anne a little, so her orange fur wouldn't carry the stains since she was too feeble to clean herself. He drove supplies from one end of the site to another, all day long, and Ms. Anne kept him company. Before he began his duty of driving supplies from one end of the site to another, Duncan would gather Ms. Anne from her bed on the front step of the foreman's trailer, put her in the truck where she could readjust her arthritic joints, and then start loading.

The construction site was already starting to look like a ballpark. Four acres of hundred-year-old pine trees came down to make room for the new high school stadium. There was a definite diamond shape happening. Gravel and red dirt covered the ground and stacks of steel beams and cinder blocks formed a maze, which Duncan had to maneuver just to get one heap of lumber from the future parking lot to the dugout. The place was a wreck from the start and would always be one, a testament to one man's colossal failure, not Duncan's, of course. People like Duncan couldn't have colossal failures. People like Duncan were scarecrows; they startle you until you realize they're just made of straw and just when you're safe, the wind blows, and he falls right on top of you. People like him had friends like Ms. Anne. Today was a little different.

Puddles from last night's rain made clay of the ground, a sucking red earth that held footprints like a seeded plum. Duncan could feel that puddle water in his mouth making his spit loose the way nickels do, like sucking on a wedding ring, still on a finger, of a stranger. The sky was ugly, unapologetically dull, a viscous, purple unwhite; it was nearly beautiful that day. There was always shit on the sidewalks around the construction site, dog/people/bird shit, a smorgasbord, a buffet really, little shit cakes for all. That morning Duncan finished loading power tools from the storage shed in his truck and was ready to get started. After the first few times of opening your truck door and being greeted with early morning cat pee you . . . no, no, there's no getting used to it. Today was the worst day ever on the site. You wouldn't know it by the way the other guys lazed around, but the sky knew what kind of day it was. Ms. Anne was curled up in the truck when the door opened and that special reek wafted out, but this time Ms. Anne didn't blink her apologies. She didn't blink at all. Ms. Anne died that Friday morning, waiting for her friend to drive her around and occasionally stroke her head.

Duncan cleaned Ms. Anne and brought her to the foreman's office, a little trailer on cinder blocks where the pitcher's mound was going to be.

-G'morning there, Duncan, said the foreman.

-Morning, Francis, said Duncan with Ms. Anne balled in his arms as though she were napping and not dead as cold chili.

Francis adjusted the name plate on his desk that read F. Hickenbotham. He wanted the workers to call him Frank or Mr. Hickenbotham, but he wouldn't *dream* of asking them to. Francis came from Vermont, and too many liberal ideas had pummeled his sense of authority, especially with black men, which all but seven of the workers were. Francis made it a point to give all the dangerous jobs to his white workers and be as firm as a drill sergeant with them, but the others he treated like comrades, and they called him Francis. Plus Francis was a scant five feet tall, had round, soft, pink cheeks, and suffered from a peculiar disease. The man's neck seemed to be dropping onto his chest from eating too many pastrami sandwiches.

-Is Ms. Anne being a bother to you? asked Francis.

Of course, it was much, much worse than that. And sadly if there was anyone who loved Ms. Anne more than Duncan it was Francis. His head just about fell to his crotch once Duncan delivered the news. Francis declared a day of mourning for the departed Ms. Anne and asked that they prepare a casket and set aside a spot on the outfield where they would bury her. The other men nodded, and once Francis was out of sight, they threw off their hard hats and had a round of RC cola. Duncan set to work on the smallest casket he'd ever seen, which didn't take but half an hour to make. Duncan drove out to the farthest fence with Ms. Anne boxed up beside him. That wasn't depressing at all; being next to dead things can really make a person feel alive. Duncan got out and sat on the edge of the truck bed, and he, too, had himself an RC cola and watched the people go by on the sidewalk.

Duncan saw a couple of women he recognized. He must have seen them at least once a week all spring. The little brown one did something different to her hair, and she wore those white shoes Duncan liked with the silver buckle across the top. The other one was beige, gap-toothed and switchy with some tall, lime-green boots. Duncan didn't understand how she could stand having her legs all sealed up in this kind of humidity, must be miserable.

-He's looking again, isn't he, Regina? said the tall boots.

Regina was severely distracted and walked with her mouth open.

-I'm talking to you! yelled tall boots.-And close your mouth before you catch flies.

Regina obeyed.

-Arlene, I can fix it, said Regina.

-You shouldn't worry so much.

-I know, Arlene. I just know I can fix it.

-Now wait a second, said Arlene, and put her hands up. What do you mean 'fix it'?

-He's looking pretty hard today, Arlene, said Regina.

There are smoother ways to change a topic of conversation, but with Arlene the mere mention of men was enough no matter what was at hand. You could shout the word penis in a sanctuary, and Arlene would just nod without a flinch and say A-Men.

-At me?

Arlene smiled and swung her backside out to the left, then to the right.

-He's looking at me, huh? asked Arlene.

-I guess. You know he's your type not mine. You like those lanky, yellow Negroes.

-Sho, you right.

Arlene turned her head and laughed with her tongue sticking out so only Regina could see.

-You are so nasty, smiled Regina.

Regina knew well enough that Arlene was not as sleazy as the space in her teeth suggested.

-Arlene, I bet you five that he doesn't say anything just like always, said Regina, perking up a bit.

Arlene stopped hard in her boots utterly dumbfounded as she swung Regina around on her heels. For a sweet moment Regina's shoes ceased filing down a raw callus on the knuckle of her middle toe. That pain was like a second consciousness to Regina, always speaking the truth, so she just learned to ignore it.

-You never stop, do you? asked Arlene.

-What?

Arlene shook her head, took a deep breath, patted the side of her curly Afro wig and walked the twenty feet or so toward Duncan. Duncan wondered why tall boots was walking his way without the silver buckles.

-Hi, said Arlene. I'm Arlene Townsend. My girlfriend and I go to Palmers Nursing Institute. We see this place all the time from there, and *hear* it.

She speared out her hand then let the wrist soften once Duncan took hold. He hesitated because he didn't really want to touch her.

-Sorry about my messy hands, he said. I'm Duncan, Duncan P. Hanks. It does get noisy.

-Hanks, huh? Are you one of the Ashton Hankses?

Arlene meant the questions as a compliment. The Ashton Hankses were a well-known and well-off black family in the area; Super Negroes is what Regina called them. A family of eleven: nine girls, two boys, and an exhausted mother who never showed the slightest hint of fatigue. She wore the fanciest hats in all of Texas, maybe in all of the country, and not just on Sundays like sane women. She wore them all the time, to the grocery store, the gas station, the doughnut shop. These were no ordinary fancy hats, these were enough to rival Queen Elizabeth's, and Mrs. Ashton Hanks strutted around like she was the unclaimed bastard child of the royal family with a big secret and a lot of money to keep it quiet. The father gave up being a surgeon to start a restaurant chain. The chain did so well that most people with a certain kind of mind conveniently forgot it was black owned.

-No, not the Ashton Hankses, he said, still worrying about silver buckles.

-Well Ashton Hanks's sister was my piano teacher for . . . for too long, she laughed.

-My daddy was Brigham Hanks. Farmer.

Well said. As much as Arlene didn't mind the idea of hard work, somehow she'd developed a clear and distinct opinion on people who were born into farming families. They were crazy. Not just plain, everyday crazy but tight-fisted, hard, and prone to unnecessary and inconvenient addictions.

-Farmer? repeated Arlene as if Duncan may have said "serial killer" or "arsonist."

-Regina! Arlene called out over her shoulder.-My friend, Regina, over there, her family *farmed*, too.

The narrow lip of Duncan's hard hat shaded his eyes. He could see the silver buckles walking their way.

-Okay, man, said Arlene, dropping the coquettish façade and getting down to business now that she was dealing with farm stock. Are you going to start speaking or am I going to have to find another way home? You say hi to my friend, all right, just for today, ordered Arlene.

And there she was. Regina paused next to Arlene and had to adjust her collar from the wind that kicked it up so her lapels kept swatting her in the chin.

-Hello, I'm Duncan.

He took off his hat, which left a ridiculous bowl mold on his short 'fro. Arlene sniggered to herself while Regina reached out her hand. Her wrist wasn't all licorice weak; it was solid considering how small she was. Regina was close enough to get a good look at Duncan for the first time. His eyes were whiteless, almost, shiny and totally black like grape jelly or some soft, watery skin from a deep sea creature against his butter-toned face. Those black, jelly eyes looked down at Regina, noticing her teardrop dimple on one side, the left, and those teeth. The front two teeth kicked back in an angle toward her tongue while the others sat normally as if they pretended not to notice the irregularity of their neighbors. They were actually useful teeth even though Regina never used them for what they were truly designed for, peeling carrots.

-I'm Regina. Nice to meet you, Duncan.

Once Regina and Arlene were away from the construction site and nearly to their destination, Arlene turned on her heels in front of Regina and bumped that sore toe.

-Where's my money? asked Arlene.

-You know that was cheating!

-*That* was not cheating," said Arlene calmly. That was life!

-All right, all right, I've learned the big lesson, mocked Regina, waving her hands in surrender. I'll owe you.

-Yeah, me and all the rest of Texas.

-That's not funny, Arlene.

-Am I laughing?

No, no, she wasn't.

The next Monday after the weekend Regina and Arlene walked the usual route from the college to the Waffle Palace #11 and to the dorm. The space between dorm and Waffle Palace #11 is where the ballpark was being built. Working at Palmers Nursing Institute paid next to nothing. Rooms were free, but food was scarce. The other students usually lived off peanuts and cola so they could afford new clothes once a week. Arlene and Regina could sew, so they ate up their money and made their clothes.

On the way to Waffle Palace #11, Duncan actually stopped Regina and Arlene.

-Would you two like to get together later today, if you're not too busy with your studies? he asked.

Arlene was so delighted that it was hard to discern Regina's lack of exuberance over the immediate yeses and we'd love tos being cast around. Regina was too hungry, and it was too early in the morning to say no to anything.

-I have to get back to work, but I'll meet you in front of those big, fancy wood doors of the institute. How's that?

-That's just fine, said Arlene, unveiling her gapped teeth in all their divided splendor.

-You think those doors are fancy, thought Regina, she smiled, and Duncan took that as a yes also.

-Welcome to Waffle Palace #11, said the waitress.

Usually the waitresses were civil, almost nice, early in the morning, and it was a gradual decline of hospitality as the day wore on, but this waitress, no matter what time of day, had her bitch hat screwed on tight.

-Oh, she said, recognizing Arlene and Regina. I'll be right back.

Arlene and Regina always ordered the same thing every morning. Sometimes they would switch plates, but it was always the same two orders coming to the table. Still, Arlene liked to be asked.

-I hate her so bad, said Arlene.

-At least we don't have to bother placing the same old order.

-That's just it. I didn't want the same old order. Mr. Ashton Hanks needs to rethink his hiring methods.

Waffle Palace #11 was actually the twelfth chain restaurant built by the Hanks family. The first one had a semitruck smash into it, one cook died but all of the patrons survived. To customers that was what mattered. So when the next Waffle Palaces sprang up, the customers kept on coming. Every Waffle Palace had the same décor, Halloween colors. Black and orange everywhere—on the tables, on the napkins, on the waitresses. They each wore a polka-dotted ascot around their necks twisted to the side with a little sass.

Regina looked up and out of her sleep fog.

-Yes, you do, she said.

-That's not the point, argued Arlene. What if I didn't today? What if, Regina?

The presumptive waitress returned with her smile still at home and juice and coffee in each hand. She promised to be back with the rest of their order and soon did just that.

-Where do you think a man like that goes after work? asked Arlene over her grits and sausage.

There was something unnatural about Arlene's ability to be so fully awake every morning without any sort of mild stimulants.

-I think he's touched in the head, said Regina, pouring syrup on her bacon.

Arlene cast a spray of grits out from between her front teeth.

-Don't say that. He's nice. And he likes you, of all people.

That's good of her, really good that Arlene is pseudo-sleazy but not stupid. She realized Duncan's disinterest in her right away, but, hey, going out is going out.

-He's not touched, but then again if he's studying *you*, a man would have to be . . .

Regina aimed her fork at Arlene, who smiled and snapped a bite of toast.

That night Duncan took Regina and Arlene to the only place he went, ever, beside work and home. The place had a good spot among the shit buffet strip not far from the ballpark site, which was good since Duncan didn't have a car. Water-stained brick and scratched windows painted over in an oily dark green summed up the curb appeal. Clumsy brushstrokes were still visible on the windows where menu items had been written in pink and blue chalk. The red leather awning was dried out and crumbling like cornflakes in the wind. Regina felt something brush her face and twitched.

-It's an old bar, whispered Regina to Arlene.

She was more than slightly dismayed and very bad at whispering.

-It's not so bad inside, said Duncan reassuringly.

-It's fabulous, said Arlene throwing up a fake smile that was more convincing than Regina's steady scowl.

-You've been to worse places and you know it, said Arlene in an actual effective whisper.

Duncan opened the weather-beaten wood door and ushered the ladies inside. Well, Duncan was no liar. It wasn't so bad inside, meaning it wasn't worse than stained walls and shit-strewn sidewalks.

-It's clean, said Regina.

There was a little relief in her voice.

-Will you stop it! ordered Arlene in her quietest shouts.

The bartender stood behind the counter with a single lightbulb positioned directly over his head like the sword of Damocles ready to strike.

-Well now, our boy Unc has some lady friends, said the bartender who possessed the most nauseating smile; it made you just want to cry. The lips were uneven and never matched the emotional projection the owner intended. Just then he was sincerely happy to see Duncan but looked like he'd been told his mother died.

-Buford owns the place, said Duncan, guiding the group over to stools at the counter.

The rest of the place was generally spare, three tables with candle bowls on each for light. Everything was so poorly lit that there was no guarantee that it was clean at all, except it smelled like soap, cigarettes and soap. Buford smiled his unright smile, lips protruded outward and didn't quite make the curve upward.

-What can I get you for? Buford asked.

-Do you have a menu? asked Arlene.

-Uh, sho do, he said.

-Really? said Duncan.

-Quiet, Unc. I'm doing business.

Buford shuffled around under the counter and pulled out two menus on plain, wrinkled paper, a little dingy with age. Regina's copy had a half-circle stain from the bottom of a wine bottle.

-You sure have a lot to offer, said Arlene.-I'll have the fried chicken and mashed potatoes with gravy.

-The same, said Regina.

Duncan scratched his head and asked if he could have a look at one of the menus. Regina passed hers to him. Regina is a pretty one, he thought, not fussy; it was like she didn't even give a damn. He planned to tell her that, in just those words, "you look like you don't even give a damn." Her skin's not one whole color, kind of golden on the cheeks and between the eyes. Buford always had it so blindingly dark in there. Most nights Duncan appreciated that, since all there was to see was Buford. Turn the lights down as much as you feel like in that case. But Duncan knew Regina in bright sun, squinting a little as she passed by him. She looked good with everything lit up like that.

-All this time I had no idea you could do all this, said Duncan, pretending to have looked at the menu.

-Well, said Buford, his sad smile drooping a little. I can't exactly make fried chicken tonight. You see I don't exactly have any chicken on hand.

-You don't have any chicken? blurted out Arlene. What you got in the kitchen then?

Buford swallowed.

-I don't exactly have a kitchen.

Regina laughed, and Duncan put his hand to his chin at the sound of it. Arlene was less than amused.

-How are you going to make any food if you don't have a kitchen? Arlene was not asking a question. She was making a clear and factual statement.

-Well, I had to sell it, you know. I still have the room back there, but, you know, the stove is gone and the oven, of course. They were connected.

-"They were connected," Arlene repeated in disbelief.

-I have the refrigerator!

-Be nice, Arlene, said Regina.

-Be nice! I'm all set to have some fried chicken, and he's talking about "I have the refrigerator!" I don't want to hear that.

-Pretzels! said Duncan like he'd discovered electricity.

Buford scrambled behind the counter again and retrieved, yes, a fresh bag of pretzels.

-Look, Arlene, said Regina. Pretzels. I bet you haven't had a pretzel in a while.

Buford eagerly poured a bowl out for each of them. The squeak from the glue breaking on the seal of the bag was like nails on a chalkboard to Arlene.

-You better take those damn pretzels out of my face.

Buford retracted Arlene's bowl of pretzels in a hurry, spilling a few on the counter. Regina couldn't help it any longer and laughed full out.

-What *do* you have here? asked Regina, once she calmed.

-Buford's got anything you can think of to drink, said Duncan, and of course . . .

Duncan lifted his bowl, and Regina nodded.

-Arlene will have a whiskey sour, said Regina while Arlene continued to fume.

-and you, Miss? asked Buford.

Regina ordered water, and Duncan a cola. She reluctantly talked about her life at Palmer's Nursing Institute. Regina wasn't a lover of bodies, other people's bodies, and that's what they were asking, no, telling her to do. Love other people's bodies; it was almost surreal to think of it really. She finally got around to asking his age.

-Twenty-nine, said Duncan.

-Good God! said Regina. I didn't think you were that old.

-Neither did I until now, said Duncan.

Duncan's Adam's apple felt a little heavier. Regina didn't apologize, she just did the quick calculation and declared him seven years older than she was, which seemed like an exorbitant figure.

-Just stood there, passing out menus like it's just . . . mumbled Arlene before finishing off her second drink.

Gradually, a few more patrons entered, most went straight through the bar to a back room. All of a sudden Duncan felt like he forgot how to talk. Sure he was saying things, but none of it made sense to him, but Regina was smiling, that was something. Duncan was afraid the words were going to stop—him, Buford, Arlene, and then there would be nothing. Nothing is never good. A friend of Duncan's came through the door, which from the distance seemed too small for him. Still he passed through easy like Santa Claus down a chimney. He was a squishy kind of man with a marshmallowy body and hair that gave his head the flowered shape of a just-baked muffin.

-Church! said Duncan.

Duncan left the squeaky stool seat to greet his buddy. Standing next to the plump friend, Duncan looked irregularly long and narrow and Church abnormally wide like two funhouse mirror versions of a normal-sized man. Regina thought how nice it is for two men to make each other so happy just by showing up. She could see that Church was the kind of person who could do that.

-Church won't be with us much longer, said Buford.

-Are you sick? asked Arlene, too pissed off to mind a natural courtesy of not accusing a person of being terminally ill.

-No, no, laughed Duncan. Church is moving to California.

-Yeah, I think a change of scenery might do me some good. I tried to get ol' Unc to head out with me, but there's no budging him. You be fair warned, young lady, he said to Regina. He's hard headed.

-Like a rock, said Buford.

-What the hell kind of name is Church? asked Arlene, finally surrendering to the pretzels.

-Well, *Hello,* Miss, said Church kindly.

He readjusted the waist of his pants.

-I'm Charles Urchin, he said. I was a minister for the better part of my life, so people call me Church.

-You must have been a young preacher then, said Regina.

-Began when I was twelve years old, Miss.

-What made you fall off the boat? asked Arlene.

Duncan smiled, so did Buford unfortunately.

-Aw, you're going to make him feel bad, said Duncan.

-Change of scenery, huh, said Arlene. What makes a person go hundreds of miles for nothing but a change of scenery?

-Oh, I just need a little of this and a little of that, but this time it'll be for good. No more Houston for me.

-That I understand.

-You keep your little California, said Buford. I'm a Texan for L-I-F-E.

-Christ, he can spell, said Arlene.

Church smiled.

Regina kept watching the men come through the door and speed right through to the back room.

-That back room must be packed tight as a sausage by now, said Regina. What's back there so interesting?

-Nothing too fascinating, mumbled Buford.

Nothing, that was just the wrong word to say to Regina. Nothing as everybody knows is everything. The most inexplicable, wonderful something that can never be thoroughly explained is always nothing. Regina slid off her squeaky stool and said,

-I want to see.

-They're just shooting craps tonight, said Duncan. It's just a game you play with dice.

-Craps, repeated Regina, her eyes glossy and heart palpitating.

-Regina, Arlene chided.

-Come on, *Unc*, said Regina.

She took his hand and quickly let go. Regina put both arms behind her back like she was hiding something. Duncan's arm was still in the air as if Regina was still holding on; it stayed there for a while all by itself. With her chin Regina motioned to the back room and led Duncan over. The back room boiled with the odor of sweat and sour pork fat. Men in suits, men in overalls, men shirtless from the body heat in the room huddled over a strip of once-blue linoleum in the middle of the floor that led to a piece of wall, the cleanest piece. The square, rust and grease stain where the old stove used to be glowed like a secret passageway. An industrial-sized vent hung over that block stain. Arlene and Church entered behind the two.

-I suppose there's no harm in watching, said Duncan.

-Unc and I never play, said Church.

-You must have other vices then, said Arlene, sucking her teeth and patting her wig coyly, but it really just itched like hell.

Church twitched back a smile.

-Do you know how to play? Duncan asked Regina.

Arlene sputtered a laugh that turned into a cough. Regina patted her back a little forcefully.

-I'm only a little familiar with it, said Regina.

-Well, the goal is to get a matching number when you roll the dice. Let's say you roll a two and a three . . .

-Five, said Regina.

-Right, smiled Duncan. You next want to roll the same thing, two and a three, or you want to roll a four and a one. Do you see?

-Okay, say I roll a four and a four.

-Yeah . . .

-Then I can roll a five and a three or a two and a six.

-I think she's got it, said Church.

-Oh, said Duncan, the other thing is there are certain things that you don't want to roll like a seven or eleven. If you roll those after you've set your number then you crap out. But if you roll those first you win automatically.

Regina was standing on her tiptoes to see into the huddle. One man in an olive green leisure suit with lapels wide enough to take flight plucked himself from the flock, dumped a cup of water over his face, and flew back in formation.

-How about you play a round for me so I can see?

-Regina, said Arlene in her motherly disapproving tone.

-Yes, that *is* my name, Arlene, she replied over her shoulder with her eyes still on the heap of bodies.

-This really is no place for two young ladies, said Church.

-Then maybe you and Arlene should go, said Regina.

-That's it! declared Arlene.

She snatched Regina up by the arm and pulled her out of the room, hurrying out apologies and excuses. Arlene even mustered up a good-bye for Buford before they were out of the stuffy bar and outside.

-Arlene! screamed Regina.

Regina didn't bother trying to pull away because even though she was angry with her friend she still trusted her, and Arlene was just physically much stronger than Regina, and the whole struggle would be utterly futile.

-Arlene, will you wait for a second!

They were minutes from the dorm, and Arlene wasn't stopping. The dorm facilities occupied the upper two floors of a square, rose-pink lunch box of a building that wore the adobe style façade like a too-big sombrero. Tonight the pink faded to a cornflower blue in the dark. Arlene tugged Regina all the way through the security gate, up the stairs and as soon as they were both inside their room, Arlene snatched off her wig and flung it behind her as if the wig was what she'd been pissed off at the whole time. Damn wigs. She aimed for her bed, but it landed on the lamp. The lamp's bulb had been on for hours and was hot as the freckles that glowed on Arlene's face.

-I can't believe you sometimes, began Arlene. As much trouble as you pretend not to be in, you still don't see it.

-I see it, said Regina.

-You see you have a problem?

-Yes.

No. Regina saw a problem but not the same one Arlene referred to. Arlene stood silent with a stocking choking her skull and confining her real hair, a wiry heap of frizzy, red spaghetti curls that hung too limp to sustain a decent 'fro. Arlene exhaled and gave Regina a hug of friendship and understanding.

-We'll get you through this, said Arlene. I thought it was easy to quit gambling once you run out of money. But I guess with you it's something else. I swear Honeysuckle is a witch from the pit of hell.

Regina listened and watched the poof of hair cooking above the scorching lightbulb. A little curl of white smoke danced from the synthetic fibers doused in hairspray. The smoke continued the sway of a charmed cobra from the sound of Arlene's prattle.

-Are you listening to me? asked Arlene.

Regina had long since checked out by the time Arlene actually noticed the smell of burning plastic and chemicals. The smoke cobra entranced Regina completely.

-What is that smell? asked Arlene.

She turned around to see the first orgasmic outburst of flame that engulfed the entire wig in the span of two blinks. Arlene screamed, while Regina enjoyed the fire. It is good (sometimes) to let things burn, perhaps not in your home, but the satisfaction is undeniable. And if Regina had to pick anything out of all things she'd like to see go up in star-spangled glory, Arlene's wig was in the top five.

-Shit me! screamed Arlene as she looked for something to put out the fire.

Not a thing. There was nothing to stop this from being a major disaster. There wasn't much time left before the lamp shade caught the fire virus. Yup, and that was it. The lamp shade was smoking, too, not nearly as robustly as Arlene's wig. Now that thing knew how to burn. Arlene threw herself out of the dorm room and ran through the hall toward the stairwell. In the stairwell a tin trash can sat half-full. Arlene snatched and tugged and sweated that trash can back to the dorm where Regina was unplugging the lamp. The room turned orange from the fire, and Regina opened the window. Arlene carefully picked up the base of the lamp and for a second she held it like a torch. The Statue of Liberty—head in a stocking, eyes wide as headlights, and pissed that her hair was on fire—bent her knees and tipped her eternal flame into a trash can. The moisture of the garbage eased the fire, and Arlene ordered Regina to help her get the whole mess outside. The two lugged the burning bin down two flights of stairs and sat it in the alley near the Dumpster. As they watched the trash burn quietly, a murderous odor escaped in huge black billows of smoke, but they didn't care. Let it burn, let it all burn, thought Regina.

-You did great, Arlene.

-Shut up, Regina.

Regina hugged Arlene, which she usually did only when she knew Arlene was irritated beyond words, and the only act that would irritate her more was a hug. This time, though, Regina really meant it.

-Get off me, said Arlene.

-I love you, too.

The next afternoon Duncan called.

-I'm surprised he would call after you behaved so *raunchily*, said Arlene over Regina's shoulder near the receiver.

-That was just Arlene, said Regina. But I don't think I'm going to be able to go out tonight. I have some studying to get done today. Can I call you later maybe?

Duncan quickly agreed.

-How is Church? I think Arlene likes him. All right, that's fine. See you later, all right? Bye.

-You are a damn liar! said Arlene, pulling off her green boots at her desk chair.

-You do like Church, said Regina. He's shaped a little funny, but he seemed nice . . .

-You know that is not what I am talking about, said Arlene, her natural, weak, orange-reddish Afro hanging like moss around her ears. Studying?

-Oh, well, it can be educational, stammered Regina.

-Honeysuckle's is *not* educational. It's de-educational. I feel dumber every time I come out of the place. And I know you're dumber every time you go in it.

-I can fix it, all right, said Regina clearly, not smiling, and with a tone that punctuated the entire conversation.

Arlene said nothing further.

Now that night Regina and Arlene set off to a place called Honeysuckle's. A woman named Miss Honeysuckle was the proprietor. The building was too new to have any of the Spanish architecture but too old to look like anything more than a raggedy crack house. Honeysuckle's had the look, feel, smell, and cash flow of a functioning crack house. The establishment was located in a former residential community where most of the properties were rezoned for small businesses that were destined to fail in eight months. Miss Honeysuckle was definitely a successful business woman. She ran a den of ill repute on the second story and a casino on the first. She had the best bargains in town for every moral-biting activity you could think of.

-I hate this place, said Arlene as they stood in front of the building.

Weeds grew dry and tall in the hard ground there, and purple vines crept over the windows so no one could actually see in (or out). It had all the enchantment of a haunted house, but Arlene knew the kinds of ghosts that roamed those halls, and they were less than friendly.

Arlene and Regina looked like wholesome southern girls, which they were. They both knew how to cook, crochet doilies, keep their legs crossed at the ankle, and speak with the polite intonations that their accents demanded. And just like most wholesome southern girls, they could swear like hurricanes, shoot guns, hunt, fish, and had the nerve to kill a man if he made it necessary to do so. They carried switchblades in their purses and one on their hips.

Given the neighborhood, leaving Honeysuckle's was just as dangerous as getting to it, even though her patrons were relatively safe inside. Miss Honeysuckle's sons were onyx and mahogany soldiers, big as three men each, who guarded the facilities like living gargoyles. Miss Honeysuckle was no less than fifty by the time Regina discovered the delights of her casino last fall. The woman was once actually beautiful, not glossy like in the movies, but a real-life beautiful, scary almost, untouchable. Her baby picture hangs in the kitchen, which Regina had been in, only once.

Regina owed a lot of money, and just last week Miss Honeysuckle demanded payment. Regina was brought into the kitchen by one of the oak soldiers where Miss Honeysuckle was eating. She saw the fading picture on the wall of a toddler posed in front of a young banana tree, and though it took some strain of the eye, Regina saw the resemblance. The high cheekbones and glistening, black almond eyes, the pouting mouth that doesn't ever seem to close all the way—

that was Miss Honeysuckle, except now she was an ex-prostitute turned pimp with a face like a gingersnap and the arms of a heavyweight boxer.

-Time to pay, said Miss Honeysuckle through greasy lips as she sat at a pretty place mat with a lace napkin and a half-spent candle unlit on the table.

-Give me one chance to earn it back, said Regina, armpits drizzling sweat. Her hands shook so hard, and she had to pee so badly that she pinched herself to stay distracted. Maybe the pain would feel better than that fear.

-You're going to earn back two thousand, four-hundred . . . Miss Honeysuckle glanced at a piece of paper beside her plate with her miraculous eyes that were growing a blue rim from old age and cataracts. Two thousand four-hundred and seventy-nine dollars.

-I can try, please, just one chance, begged Regina. She actually lost herself and reached out and touched Miss Honeysuckle's crocodile-tail arm.

Miss Honeysuckle smiled and said yes. Five days was the set time. Regina earned enough money from her job at the Institute to play the games and try to double up. Arlene picked up the check at Waffle Palace #11. Regina only needed to double her check about seventeen times. No problem.

-Come on, said Regina.

The spicy smell of all that busy ass from the second floor was enough to make a person dizzy, nasal hazards of a special work environment like rendered meat at a slaughtering house or rotten eggs at a sulfur mine. The two passed by the pair of bouncers like ladybugs over elephants. Arlene spotted Sylvia, who was on a usual break. Sylvia was not much older than these two and wore pink clam diggers and a green bra with nothing else. She wasn't fat but was flabby around the middle so her gut slumped over the waistband of her clam diggers. Arlene and Regina often talked to some of the working girls, the ones who would talk and not scowl at them for not being paying customers. Arlene spent all of her time there talking to Sylvia, and that was not easy. Talking to Sylvia was like trying to strike a match in the wind, usually worth it but no guarantees. She flickered in that way, off and on, sometimes she would get the dead-eye, and that was it. Arlene would be quiet and just sit there next to her in that stank hallway beneath a single iron sconce. Indentured servitude to Miss Honeysuckle had some perks. You never really had to be the one putting in the hours. You could mentally disappear. Maybe Honeysuckle trained them to do it that way. Most of the working girls named themselves after fruit: peaches, honeydew, strawberry delight, cantaloupe. Cantaloupe was a big girl. So when your time was up, and if you wanted out, you could part ways with Honeysuckle's and leave peaches behind. It was a nice strategy, in theory. Not Sylvia. Her working name was actually Sylvia. She had a daughter at fifteen, born with a club foot, now living in Arkansas under the grandmother's care. The father, Billy, was thirty-four and stocked shelves in a drugstore. He was caught stealing baby-rash lotion when the tube burst down the front of his pants. Harold, the manager, was deeply flattered for a moment, but soon commenced to pound Billy like he stole something, then the strangled tube of ointment fell out of his pants, and Harold realized Billy really was a thief and not a pervert. Sylvia's mother said she was cursed, said she'd cripple everything she touched, her men and even her children. So Sylvia fled to Texas, whored herself for food and shelter, and eventually was discovered by Miss Honeysuckle, who had an eye for talent indeed.

Miss Honeysuckle occupied the only rooms other than the casino (a hollowed-out living room and a den) that had electricity or a telephone, which is really cost efficient. What separated Honeysuckle's from the other city hot spots was simple, no drugs. She didn't sell them, and she wouldn't have them in her establishment. No exceptions. Most whores had honor, but the average crack-whore will rob you blind and blow your Rottweiler for a five dollar fix. No drugs. In fact, anyone on the premises with a disagreeable substance was immediately pitched out on their necks.

Maybe that was the appeal the place had for Regina. Beyond the reasonable game prices, there was a cleanliness of mind. Regina naturally dismissed the tainted intentions, but she was too distracted at the crap table. She hadn't been able to get the taste of craps out of her mouth since she was torn from the game at Buford's place. Damn Arlene always playing mama, thought Regina. She had the dice in hand now. Only a few women ever showed up, usually with their male partners, but most brought a male partner who watched as they gambled. Since Regina was more alone than that, she caught most of the witty comments and occasionally strokes of her backside, which were answered appropriately. A tiny fist in the nuts. Honeysuckle's boys always came like spirits and ferried the assailant away.

-Seven! someone shouted.

Regina was off to a good start. She'd doubled up half her check.

-Seven!

Nice. But she wasn't getting too happy yet. She knew she had to earn it.

-Seven!

What the hell?

-Them dice is fixed! yelled a man with a little girl's voice.

-Four.

Okay, okay, Regina could do four, two and two, one and three.

-Five.

The four is still out there, it's still good.

-Five.

Not a problem. Two and two, one and three.

-Seven!

Damn it! That's all right. The sevens want to come up, let them come up. Regina had it worked out; she'd put it all up now while the sevens are hot, double up fast and have room to maneuver. That'll do it. Arlene peeked inside for just a second and couldn't stand to look on. Regina took the sweaty dice in her left hand. Wait, double up?! Regina was going to lose it all quick, fast, and in a hurry. What did Honeysuckle do to those who couldn't pay their debts again? Regina asked herself. Regina wasn't stupid, she knew good and well that there was a cot upstairs with her name on it, whatever she decides to call herself: chocolate drop, blackberry surprise.

-Eight!

Four and four, five and three, six and two. A greasy hand was rubbing up Regina's thigh, and she didn't even feel it. Not until she let the dice fly did the hand go up a little too far. Regina spun around to see a frog-eyed man with an evil grin kneeling under her. She instantly proceeded to choke him out. The crowd turned to watch the skirmish before the dice even hit the felt. Regina was a click away from pulling out the switchblade when Honeysuckle's goons entered. They lifted her gingerly like a potted plant while she flailed about.

-Seven!

No. The dice were scooped up before Regina could see, and she was hauled out of the room.

-Regina! yelled Arlene. Put her down! What happened?

-I'm okay, Arlene," said Regina calmly, her head inches from the ceiling. Wait for me, I'll be right back.

She said it as though she were off to the ladies room. She looked more like a human sacrifice about to be offered up to some old, sadistic demigod. Regina was deposited into a chair at the kitchen table where Miss Honeysuckle waited. Miss Honeysuckle crossed her rhinoceros thighs with the smile of a Venus flytrap holding a cockroach behind her teeth. The lovely baby girl in the photograph on the wall covered her ears, and those delicate almond eyes were now only charcoal slivers. She did not smile.

Regina drew her legs under the chair and straightened her shoulders as Miss Honeysuckle said her name.

-Are you ready? asked Miss Honeysuckle.

Miss Honeysuckle had a voice like chicken soup or meatloaf, a mother's voice.

-May I have a day to collect my things? asked Regina, tracing the blue eel circling Miss Honeysuckle's eye, sucking on its tail.

-Certainly.

How generous! Miss Honeysuckle was indeed a pimp with a heart. This wouldn't be so bad. Regina had only to work off her debt, and then it would be like this never happened. Regina expressed her gratitude and—goodness—she nearly smiled.

-My boys will meet you tomorrow evening at that nursing school if you aren't back by then to help you with your things, of course.

Regina passed through the doorway, which was blocked by Miss Honeysuckle's sentinels. Regina slid through them like a mouse through a crack and found Arlene waiting in the foyer.

-What the hell was that?! asked Arlene.

Regina answered frankly but strongly. She reassured Arlene that everything had been put in order, and she would do what she had to do. Arlene cried and put her head on Regina's shoulder as they walked through the streets back to the dorm. That's how Regina played it out in her mind the first few steps out of Honeysuckle's, but in reality she'd been stone silent and blank faced for too many seconds. They continued for a few more feet under the barely dark sky. It didn't take long for Regina to tie her noose and make the leap. Arlene opened her mouth to ask again and got a flicker of the dead-eye in Regina's face. Arlene slapped her. She slapped her kind of hard though, but she had to make it go away.

-You didn't, breathed Arlene.

-I'll be all right, said Regina.

-You'll be all right!

Arlene stopped Regina by the shoulder and shook her like a bad babysitter.

-You'll be all right!!

-Arlene, said Regina, her voice vibrating. Arlene—please—stop.

Finally Arlene tired herself out and pulled Regina toward her for support. Arlene was just about too weak to stand on her own, and Regina held her up by the waist.

-God damn you, Regina.

The air didn't smell like shit. It smelled like Arlene, all hairspray and fried chicken.

-I think so.

Duncan ate six bowls of pretzels and one RC cola, one for each bowl of pretzels. He was just recovering from passing out the second time.

-You ain't gon' shit right for a week, said Buford under that unflattering lightbulb.

Duncan didn't care, the salt and sugar made him happy, happy meaning bloated, gaseous, cranky, and dizzy. He felt drunk without the side effect of feeling out of control. He still had sense enough to know where his wallet was and who he was talking to, but he was distracted enough by his body not to think about what he kept thinking about.

-Stop thinking about that girl, man, said Buford. I haven't seen a man fall over backward for a woman since that movie.

-Which movie? burped Duncan.

-The one with them legs, said Buford, rubbing the oil from his forehead with the back of his wrist,-you know, the broad with them legs.

Duncan shrugged. The door opened, and the night actually brought some light into the place instead of pulling it out. No one occupied the tables, the only candlelight came from the wick next to Duncan's latest bowl of pretzels. Two men, one familiar, one not.

-Duncan!

-Hey, Church, he replied, half-heartedly.

Church and the stranger came to the bar. Buford mixed up some fancy gin potion for the stranger without even asking.

-Duncan, you look like death, said Church. Are you still tore up about Ms. Anne?

-Aww, shut up, Church, said Buford. He ain't fretting that cat!

Well, Duncan wasn't thinking about Ms. Anne until Church mentioned her. Thanks for that pleasant thought, just one more living thing that didn't want to be around him.

-It's his girl, said Buford.

-The one you just met? said Church.

-One of the two you were with before? asked the stranger.

Who does this guy think he is, talking to Duncan like he knows him, like he's family? Why don't you shut the hell up, cousin? Duncan thought.

-Yeah, yeah, said Duncan, more than annoyed at the random man.

-I'm trying to tell him, said Buford, the way they shot out of here like someone branded them in the ass. Looks to me like they ain't interested.

Buford was probably right, for the first time in his life. Regina wasn't interested. Blew him off for "*studying.*" She's smart and has all those young college . . .

-Sometimes I think ol' Duncan will never find a girl, said Church,- then two seconds later you're talking like she's *the* one. What do they call them?

-Regina, said Duncan.

-No, waved Church. He rubbed a hand over his muffin 'fro. Buford, you know what I'm talking about. When two people are, you know, when they're tied together.

-Hostages, said Buford.

-No! I mean when they're made from heaven together, and then they bust up along the way to earth and then they try to find each other.

-Soul mates, said the stranger, and I don't know if you want to make those two anybody's soul mates.

Duncan finally pulled his head out of the pretzels to see this aggravating man.

-Be careful, said Duncan.

Church cleared his throat and told the stranger to go on to the back and play some games, but the stranger finally had someone's undivided attention and wasn't letting go just yet.

-I just saw both of them, he said, fingering his half-a-chocolate-doughnut mustache, both the dark one and the light one over at Honeysuckle's.

-What? said Buford in slow motion.

Duncan stood up, not exactly a big man, but certainly tall, and certainly strong, and certainly that was enough to make the stranger hop a yard or two in reverse.

-I'm just saying as a warning to *you*, friend, said the stranger. If she's on Honeysuckle's payroll, I wouldn't go stitching my soul to her just yet.

The stranger made it through the door to the back room after spilling a few sloshes of gin.

-What's he know, said Duncan. Just wants a fight is all.

Buford nodded, but Church was quiet. Duncan snapped his neck in Church's direction, awaiting confirmation, but it wasn't coming.

-Did you see? asked Duncan, the sleep in his eyes cracking apart.

Church nodded. Jesus, Regina was a working girl. Working for Miss Honeysuckle! She lied to him. Regina smiled in his face, touched his hand, she laughed like he couldn't believe, and she's out shucking her goods for fifty bucks, he figured.

Well, fifty was a little pricey, but Duncan—God bless him—would have paid fifty, paid it every day, for the rest of his life. But now, Regina, poor thing, was nothing more than a gold doubloon that turned out to be full of chocolate that turned out to be a molded turd. Duncan sat back down, he slumped over so completely that the bricks of his spine ridged through his shirt. He looked into an arc of spilled cola on the counter and said a word; it wasn't quite declarative like he does when he's discovered something undeniably plain yet tremendously important, still it was close enough.

-California.

-Have a late lunch with me? asked Regina while she folded clothes on her bed.

-Sure, said Arlene, watching Regina pack.

Arlene had been up all night trying to figure a way out of this, but every plan Regina shot down like it was hunting season. The police? They're too slow. The school? They don't care.

-Call your mother, for God's sake!

Regina laughed at that one. Even though Regina was an only child, her parents were notoriously wrapped up in their own warring worlds to bother with her in any way beyond food and shelter and only then if she was in the immediate vicinity. Still, Regina actually managed to sleep well that night. It was amazing how she could do that, just paint the world the way it should be in her mind, all sugarplums and fairies then just close her eyes and go live there for eight hours straight. All the while Arlene kept seeing Sylvia and her eyes.

-I have to withdraw from the Institute properly, so I can come back without a big fuss, said Regina.

She was going on vacation. Arlene knew that's how Regina was seeing things. Regina was taking a year off, maybe two, to travel the world. She was off to see the pyramids, get spat on by camels and buried to her neck in a sandstorm. She was going to swim in the

Amazon and get stung by a wasp the size of her head and be stricken with fever; in her delirium she was going to ride a three-headed unicorn over a field of rusty teaspoons, growing on the tails of mayonnaise comets in an empty heaven, breathing the shedding skin of near-dead planets, deeply. She was going to drink ground papaya seeds mixed with the saliva of a witch doctor and recover. She was going to climb the Himalayas wearing a thirty-pound Yak fur coat, break her ankle in the snow and be nursed back to health by monks; she was going to shave her head and learn to chant prayers for days at a time; she was going to stow away onboard ships and flirt with men in kilts; she was going to plant rice paddies and master the art of guerrilla warfare; she was going to hide in the trees with coconuts and grenades, while the migrained soldiers wonder who keeps dropping those damn coconuts; she was going to bury her elbows in blue-black sand, watching tiny spotted lizards mate between her toes.

Arlene wanted that, too. As close as she wanted Regina nearby, she wanted Regina far, far away, where she would have good reason to buy postcards. Yes, that's it, thought Arlene. They would *both* be insane that morning. It was such a delightful day for dementia. The clouds were at a breathable distance from one another, each gloriously white, never interrupting the sun's rays for longer than was polite. Regina's suitcase snapped shut.

Arlene was thinking so hard that her mouth fell open. Regina turned and came over to Arlene's side of the room. Regina closed Arlene's mouth with her palm, hugged her head, and kissed that pitiful hair.

-Meet me at three, said Regina.

-Sure.

The door opened, closed, and was locked from the outside.

Regina strolled her delusional self on into Waffle Palace #11 at ten to three that afternoon. She was a little early so she wasn't surprised not to see Arlene yet. A corner booth with a view of the street was open. Regina smiled at the waitress who was already looking tired, rubbing the back of her calf with her foot. It was a different waitress than in the mornings. Great legs, thought Regina as she slid into the seat, but that face. It is more than a little jarring when you see a young person from behind, all smooth legs and firm body, and when they turn around it's like their face melted in some kind of freak accident when in actuality they're just old. The waitress was like that, and Regina felt the first of many pangs of sadness when she realized the old-faced woman had no name. Regina never asked, never glanced at the orange nameplate on her breast, all the months Regina had eaten at that restaurant in the afternoon.

Thirty-three minutes after three o'clock, Regina finished two iced teas and was still alone. No Arlene. What's that about? What kind of friend would . . . okay, no, something must have happened to her. She's just late.

"Can I have another tea, please?" Regina ordered.

-Sure, sweetie.

Ahhh! Her voice was old, too. Regina wondered if they did head transplants now. She thought how nice that would be if she could have one of those today, just give her body to somebody else for a while. She'd even take an old body, especially one like the waitress's. She'd take a man's body for that matter. But now she was thinking about Duncan, and there came another pang. Duncan might do something like that, switch bodies with her. Arlene, too, wherever the hell she was. But Regina would hug a moving train before she let that happen. It would be nice to do that, to hug him; she hadn't done that with Duncan. Regina wanted to hug a man today, a man that mattered, since she would have a whole string of them that didn't mean a thing. It was twenty minutes to five o'clock when her appetite was thoroughly destroyed by Arlene's absence. Regina couldn't stand to eat anything. Her bladder was full of tea and ached like a sprained joint, but Regina didn't care. She wasn't going to pee. Damn some pee! She was going back to her dorm to wait for her future.

Regina passed two students in the hall who said hello, but she could only muster a half smile and a nod.

-Cramps, Regina heard one of them say.

The nerve of some people, always thinking they know exactly what's going on. They can sum up a whole life with one word. Regina reached for her keys inside her purse and realized she was holding her waist rather uncomfortably. Three iced teas along with her nervous state equaled one lightning-fast trip to the restroom, which was really a close call. The dorm bathrooms were only two doors down.

Regina came back and sat on top of her suitcase, knitting a handkerchief with some huge rods obscenely referred to as needles. They were Arlene's, and even though Regina couldn't crochet worth a damn, she could knit fairly: mostly handkerchiefs, placemats, square things. The click of the needles and relief in her bladder made all the world right again. Regina would accept her duty peacefully. She contemplated what her new name would be: flowers. Regina could be a flower. Hibiscus, maybe? What the hell does that look like anyway? It sounds like high biscuits—too suggestive. Narcissus? Regina wouldn't dare have that many S sounds in her name. Jasmine. She's always liked that. They smell nice. Maybe Camille. No, that was her mother's middle name. Or maybe that was just right? Maybe a noun, an abstract idea or something that gave the impression of one like Constance.

Regina was going to serve her time then return to the life she meant to finish. She was resolved. This wouldn't be easy, but she made up her mind. A strong knock sounded on the door. The boys had arrived. Regina . . . Regina was gone. She leapt out the window so fast her suitcase popped open. But she didn't bother bringing it with her. She left those needles spinning on the floor. No fire escape, no hidden ladder, just window sills and the possibility of broken bones. Regina scaled the side of the building like she'd been given powers from a radioactive spider. In seconds she was running around to the alley when someone called her name. Jesus! Tell the world where she was! Regina managed to get to the alley with the Dumpster, and right beside it was the trash can she and Arlene burned days ago. The Dumpster had all day to heat up under the sun and poot a sweet and tangy scent into the air that Regina must have thought quite inviting. She heaved her little body up onto the slimy edge and slipped. She meant to swing her legs over but flipped forward head first into the death stench.

"There's the girl!" a man yelled.

They were close now. They must have seen her go in. Regina pulled a sack of garbage over her like a sleeping bag, except this sleeping bag burst on her chest and out fell some rancid cauliflower and a used maxi pad. She hoped it was cauliflower. Regina was dead still, not even breathing, which was the easiest thing to do at the moment given the tossed salad of stomach-boiling aromas.

But it was no use, she was discovered. Two heads peeked over the Dumpster rim. Both were silhouetted in the evening sun, and all Regina could make out were two of the raggediest Afros she'd ever seen, one drooping and glowing with a red diadem and the other a distinct muffin . . .

-Church! yelled Regina. Arlene?

-Yes! What are you doing?

-I . . . , began Regina feebly. I ran.

Arlene never saw anything so pitiful in her life. She wanted to pick Regina up and hug her forever, but Arlene couldn't help her first instinct above all others. She laughed. Later she would laugh herself to a headache then to tears, but now she and Church helped Regina out of the trash bin.

-You never showed! said Regina, once she was on her feet and wondering what the pink-orange thing was that was sliding down her knee.

-I was busy and for good reason.

Church waved his hand.

-You better not mean what I think you mean. Busy! yelled Regina. You were out being busy with him!

-Shut up, Regina, said Arlene calmly but with a satisfied smirk. I was getting you help. Church is going to California, and so are you.

-Wait a minute," said Regina throwing up her arms.

-Shut up, Regina.

She obeyed.

-He and Duncan are . . .

-Duncan?

-If I have to tell you one more time, commanded Arlene.

Regina pressed her lips together and realized something. It was over. She'd gotten away. Well, she would have to get out of the state first, but she was done with Miss Honeysuckle, and her debt was wiped out. She would travel for the first time all the way to the West Coast with Duncan. She never thought of traveling with Duncan. He seemed so stationary. Arlene was still explaining the plan, but Regina was already prepared to give Arlene the biggest, nastiest thank you hug ever. Arlene protested for a moment but surrendered, of course.

-I'm going to miss you, goddammit, said Arlene.

-What?

Regina missed that little detail. Arlene naturally had no reason to leave. Her finances were in order, and she was scheduled to finish school in the winter. Regina's head filled with water and went deaf. Arlene was talking, but Regina could only read her lips.

-I'm not dying, she said. We're still here.

Regina nodded. Her California adventure just took a miserable turn. Arlene took Regina's keys and left her in Church's care while she went to help Duncan get her luggage. He was the one at the door and must have been waiting without a clue. Arlene and Regina hugged one last time before Regina slipped into the backseat of Church's Buick.

Arlene's voice was the last thing Regina ever remembered before leaving the city limits.

-Jesus, you smell like hell.

To order or obtain more information on these or other
University of Nebraska Press titles, visit nebraskapress.unl.edu.

CPSIA information can be obtained
at www.ICGtesting.com
Printed in the USA
LVOW03s1746310118
564753LV00004B/811/P